BOOKS

Simply Learning, Simply Best

Simply Learning, Simply Best

倍斯特出版事業有限公司
Best Publishing Ltd.

胡夢瑋 ◎ 著

啟航吧！
我的空服夢！

FLIGHT ATTENDANT

夢想啟航

空服員的英文應試＋飛行日誌

100%應試準備教戰：

➤ 【航空公司招考資訊】，一次看懂、看好、看準招募公告！

➤ 【求職信、履歷、自傳範例】，寫出主考官要的書面資料！

➤ 【自我介紹】，用英文自我介紹promote個人優勢！

➤ 【面試廣播詞】，唸對廣播詞，以備臨時抽考！

特別企劃【空服員飛行英語日記】，溫心收錄空服前輩實際在職服務的工作百態，教你／妳如何在入行後快速上手?! 碰到難搞的乘客該怎麼辦?!

強烈推薦給：空服求職新鮮人／空服從業人員／航空系師生

MP3

作者序
Preface

考空服前該做什麼？

大家常說空服員面試是一件很主觀的事情，而且還要靠一點自身的運氣。他們說的沒錯，不過在踏上戰場之前你總得知道如何戰鬥吧？在本書中，從國內外航空公司的簡單介紹、求職訊息怎麼看、到如何準備自傳和履歷、各種情境的廣播稿練習還有實際上戰場後飛行時會發生的真實狀況，都說給你聽。讓你在瞭解更多航空界的資訊後，帶著比別人更多的自信心去面試。

你有沒有常覺得英文是一種羈絆？

出國想要說英文的時候力不從心、或準備面試的時候才發現書到用時方恨少？其實英文不應該是羈絆，就像中文一樣，它是人與人溝通、表達自己的媒介。在日常生活當中，我們講的中文也不會艱澀到哪裡去。同理英文也一樣，各項的檢定考或許能知道你的英文程度到哪裡，不過實際上到國外使用或面試工作的時候又是另一回事，對方能理解你要表達的東西，才是最重要的。

因此，本書彙整外商空服員面試要點。除了介紹英文履歷、自傳撰寫的基本要素之外，透過飛機上各種空服員與乘客間的情境對話，讓讀者更了解飛機上常用字詞和外國人的日常用語，輕鬆應對飛航的不同狀況。

準備好要起飛了嗎？

只要會聽、敢講，你就可以跟我一起遨遊世界了！

胡夢瑋

編者序
Editor

　　對許多即將踏入社會的新鮮人，空服員是他們嚮往的行業；對已在職場打滾幾年的人，空服員是他們準備轉換跑道的目標。

　　網路上關於考取空服員的資訊很多，坊間也不乏專業的航空補習班，書店也販售相關的應試祕笈，但是要如何才能更有效地準備空服應試？更貼切空服的實際工作樣貌？這是我們一直在思考，也一直力求突破與進步的方向。

　　我們很幸運地找到了在外商航空公司服務的胡夢瑋老師，老師本身有豐富的本土、外商航空公司的面試實戰經驗，且已飛行超過30個國家。相信以她的經歷，必能帶給讀者更完善的資訊！

　　本書規劃了撰寫個人履歷、自傳、推薦信的技巧與範本供讀者參考；同時收錄包括男女、新鮮人、地勤轉職者和其他行業轉職者的自我介紹範本，另有機上廣播詞，供讀者練習；更特地增加了在職服務時會用上的口說英文。

　　謝謝夢瑋老師的熱情與用心！期許閱讀本書的讀者都能成功圓滿空服夢！

編輯部

使用說明
Instructions

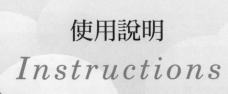

1-1 航空公司與航空聯盟簡介

收錄多家航空公司與聯盟簡介，入行前先熟知東家的特色！

✈ 中華航空空司 China Airlines

　　中華航空(China Airlines)成立於 1959 年，為台灣第一大民用航空業者並且於 2011 年加入天合聯盟成為其中會員。中華航空至今為止，共飛有 28 個國家、112 個航點，包括歐洲、美洲、大洋洲、亞洲等區域。華航的企業願景為「值得信賴，邁向卓越」，並以以熱忱感動客戶、用關懷照顧員工、用行動支持夥伴、用文化......續呵護地球以及用誠信滿足股東等六大使命著手實行，共......生共榮的未來。

(以上資料參......

✈ 長榮航空 EVA Air

　　長榮航空（EVA Air）成立於 1991 年，至今飛......洲、澳洲、歐洲及美洲等六十多個城市，並且在 2013......盟的會員之一。長榮航空以飛航安全快捷、服務親切周到......新等理念經營企業。而長榮航空最有名的 Hello Kitty 彩......航空業創新的行銷範例。另外，長榮航空也自 2004 年......得德國專業航空雜誌 Aero International 雜誌，評選......

· 16 ·

🧳 Part 1 招考資訊

是新航在發想新服務時的第一考量。

(以上資料參考新加坡航空。)

✈ Star Alliance 星空聯盟

　　星空聯盟（Star Alliance）是一個全球性的航空公司網絡，成立於 1997 年 5 月 14 日，為全球第一家航空公司聯盟。其總部位於德國法蘭克福，至今聯盟成員數已達 26 個，為現在歷史最悠久且規模最大的航空公司聯盟。星空聯盟的宗旨為「通過既定流程，建立管理、聯盟產品和服務的領導地位」。星空聯盟品牌也代表著，無論旅客位於世界何處，都盡力為他們提供順暢的旅行體驗。

　　星空聯盟間的合作方式為：共同的里程累積酬賓計畫、兼容優惠服務、「同一屋簷下」計畫、隨著全球網絡的建立協調一致的定期航班、單張機票可搭乘聯盟其他航空公司的航班、共用的航線網絡及停機位等等。而其聯盟下的航空公司包括，長榮航空（EVA Air）、新加坡航空（Singapore Airlines）、全日本空輸（All Nippon Airways）、韓亞航空（Asiana Airlines）、中國國際航空公司（Air Chian）等等。

(以上資料參考星空聯盟官方網站。)

✈ Sky Team 天合聯盟

　　天合聯盟（Sky Team）為 2000 年創立的航空聯盟，初期由法國航空、達美航空、墨西哥國際航空和大韓航空聯合成立，至今已有

· 18 ·

1-2 求職廣告怎麼看

看懂航空公司的英文徵才廣告，選到最理想的職位！

從何得知徵才消息？

在網路發達的現代生活，我們幾乎可以透過網路就得知徵才訊息，常見的不外乎網路上的人力銀行、該公司的官方網站上、朋友口耳相傳，不然就是隨著社群網站興起的粉絲團或部落格上面得知。得知徵才訊息不難，⋯⋯

員之前，就⋯⋯
司網站，亦⋯⋯
試消息一旦⋯⋯
息，會忙⋯⋯
空服員之前⋯⋯
息，才不會⋯⋯

徵才⋯⋯

大家常⋯⋯
徵才的內容⋯⋯
目的、時間⋯⋯
外，也避免⋯⋯

Part 1 招考資訊

呎高的機艙內，身體的適應力要很好，當然如果本來身體狀況比較不佳的人，公司可能就會考慮要不要雇用你。職前健康檢查通常是在全部的面試都通過之後，公司才會通知你進行健康檢查，檢查合格即可參加，受訓不合格只好下次再見。建議考生維持健康的作息，把身體調整到做好的狀態，除了在準備面試的過程中能有好心情之外，也好面對接下來的健康檢查以及受訓生活。

外商公司徵才廣告

▶▶▶ **Cathay Pacific- Flight Attendant (Hong Kong base)**
Key responsibilities:
1. Carry out inflight safety and security procedures.
2. Provide oxcellent customer service exceeding passengers expectation.
3. Anticipate and respond to passengers needs promptly and in a professional⋯⋯

Requirements:
1. Citizen of Taiwan
2. Minimum age of 18⋯⋯
3. High school gradua⋯⋯
4. Speak and read Eng⋯⋯ language is preferab⋯⋯
5. Great interpersonal⋯⋯ and customer-orient⋯⋯
6. Experienced in servi⋯⋯

7. An arm-reach of 208cm and physical fitness to pass the pre-employment medical assessment

＊Male applicants should be exempted from or have completed military service.

▶▶▶ **國泰航空—空服員（基地位於香港）**
職務：
1. 實行機上安全和保安程序
2. 提供精湛的服務品質並且超越乘客期望
3. 專業地滿足顧客需要
應徵條件：
1. 具中華民國國籍者
2. 年滿 18 歲
3. 高中畢業
4. 具備流利英語及中文能力，第三語言尤佳
5. 具良好的互動能力且有服務熱忱
6. 具備服務業經驗尤佳
7. 必須通過職前的健康檢查及 208 公分的摸高測驗

＊男性應徵者必須服完兵役或免役。

1 招考資訊

2 100%完勝準備攻略

3 交通服務機業流程筆記

4 附錄

2-1 求職信（Cover Letter）

為什麼要寫求職信？

求職信是一份附在履歷前面的自我推薦信，是一個非常精簡的自我介紹，也是主管透過紙本對你的第一印象。完成一份好的求職信，可以替你的整體印象加很多分。

求職信的目的是要讓主管透過求職信了解你應徵的動機，從龐大的應徵者信件當中脫穎而出爭取和主管面試的機會。因此，求職信表達的是你比其他人更能勝任這份工作。求職信和履歷不同的是，求職信是讓主管對你產生好的第一印象進而面試你，信中通常精簡的提到自己能夠勝任這份工作的能力、特質，履歷則是在面試之前主管可以更進一步了解你過去的學經歷和能力。

求職信裡該寫些什麼？

求職信大致上分成三個部分，包括抬頭（應徵者的姓名、聯絡方式）、正文（求職信的主要段落）以及結尾（署名）。

詳列撰寫求職信的訣竅，寫出一封誠意十足的 cover letter！

提供求職信範本做參考，下筆時文思不枯竭！

In addition to fluent English ability, I am an open minded, optimistic and cheerful person. I am a good communicator and cooperator in a team as well as helping others. According to above, I actively attend in lots of activities. In 2015, I was the translator of the International Education Expo, which helped students get more information about different colleges around the world. I was the bridge between Taiwanese student and the representatives from international colleges. Therefore, I am good at communicating as well as seeing the questions, and solving them with patience and calmness.

Last but not least, I hope I have this honor to join ABC airlines. I believe I can bring happiness on the aircraft as well as dealing with different kind of issues. Thank you for your consideration and I am looking forward to hearing from you. Within next week, I will contact you to answer any questions you may have. Thank you.

Sincerely　*Jenny Wu*
（簽名）

2-2 履歷（Resume）

傳授如何寫出好履歷的秘訣！另提供範例。

在簡單地介紹完自己之後，如果主管有興趣認識你接著就會看你的履歷。我們常常聽到的⋯⋯（Vitae）和履歷 Res⋯⋯歷 Resume，CV 比⋯⋯

CV 和 Re⋯⋯

Resume 是你⋯⋯貝，履歷的筆調是很⋯⋯驗，那麼就盡量放與⋯⋯人想要看你歷年來做⋯⋯寫即可。

Curriculum Va⋯⋯哪些事情。因此它是⋯⋯程度、學術成就、工⋯⋯份是用來申請獎⋯⋯acadamic resume⋯⋯

在歐洲、中東⋯⋯

2-2 | 履歷（Resume）

有特定的要求，通常指的就是簡歷，對 CV 和 Resume 有明確的要求主要是在美國。在美國 CV 主要是用來申請學術、教育或研究等的職位，也可申請獎學金。因此在台灣的話，應徵工作主要還是以簡歷為主。

怎麼寫履歷？

履歷主要是以一頁 A4 大小的紙清楚概要的方式列出⋯⋯和個人特質，其中包括你的個人資料、專長、學歷、經驗⋯⋯成就等等，可以依照個人學經歷或職位需求而擺放不同成就⋯⋯了掌握上述在討論求職信的書寫原則之外（包括口氣堅定詢⋯⋯簡扼要、聯絡方式、反覆校對、避免全部大寫等等），在大⋯⋯同學經歷的條件下，如何能脫穎而出讓主管雇用你，以下幾⋯⋯別注意：

1.履歷長度

履歷的長度盡量以一頁為原則，最多不超過兩頁。不要⋯⋯訴老闆你得過多少獎、參加過多少活動就把所有事蹟都放在任⋯⋯挑重要的或是與應徵工作最相關的資訊來講就夠了，不然主⋯⋯讀你的履歷的時候因為太多內容而忽略你真正想要表達的重⋯⋯

Part 2 100%應試準備教戰

履歷範例

▶▶▶ 範例一

Jessica Lin

PERSONAL DATA
Date of Birth | 01 January, 1990
Tel | +886123456789
Address | No.1, Apple Rd., Banana Township, Orange County, Taiwan.
Email | jessicalin@email.com

HIGHLIGHTS OF QUALIFICATIONS
❑ Excellent English ability of speaking, listening, writing, and reading. Capable of communicating with foreigners.
❑ A good team player and quick learner. Work easily and confidently.
❑ Great enthusiasm in helping and serving others.
❑ Great problem-solving skills and positive attitude.

2-3 自傳（Autobiography）

詳述如何寫出好自傳的訣竅！另提供範例。

在空服員徵才中通常不太需要繳交自傳，頂多是履歷跟求職信而已，不過也可能因為不同航空公司有不同的要求，因此在求職之前最好把這三樣東西一起準備起來，以備不時之需。

為什麼需要自傳？

求職信的準備是為了讓主管有興趣繼續閱讀你的⋯⋯的學經歷成就以條列式的方式展現出來，如果主管⋯⋯有好奇心會接著看你的自傳（如果有要求的話）。比⋯⋯傳更能展現個人特色，也更能表達你想告訴主⋯⋯以你應徵的職位有相關聯。

自傳怎麼寫？

一般來說自傳的長度維持在 600-800 字，並以⋯⋯不需要交代太多細節，通常維持在一頁就夠了。自傳⋯⋯由，並沒有硬性規定要寫什麼樣的內容，主要是依照⋯⋯在自己哪部份的能力或經歷，不過若是沒有頭緒，通⋯⋯書寫，而每段內容如下：自傳中第一段，通常擺放自⋯⋯過這部分簡單帶過就好不必贅述，並且盡量與自己的⋯⋯

· 60 ·

Part 2 100%應試準備教戰

自傳範例

▶▶▶ 範例一

I am Ann. Due to my father's job, my family and I moved to U.S.A for few years. Growing under American culture, not only do I have a good command of English, but I also have an open-minded, optimistic and friendly personality. I like to help others and enjoy the happiness from it.

I have a great interest in attending team activities. During my college, I had been the chief of activities of student association of our department. On the other hand, I was also the main actor in our senior year graduation play. In these activities, I learned how to help others, how to communicate and cooperate in a team. As well as having experiences in part-time job such as assistant of department, waitress in cafe, I am familiar with service industry.

During college, I used to be the interpreter of the International

2-4 面試自我介紹

✈ 自我介紹 1　　　　　　　　🎧 Track 01

Hello everyone. I'm Lisa from Taiwan. I am a student majoring in English and minoring in Spanish as well. I once lived in Sydney, Australia as an exchange student for a year. In Sydney, I made a lot of friends coming from different countries. There were Chinese, Japanese, English, Portuguese, and so on. It is so interesting when all different nationalities meet. We shared various opinions, jokes, foods, living ways and much more. I really enjoy the life there. One thing I'd learnt during the exchange program is that the world is so much more colorful with all different kinds of culture.

I love to travel while at the same time discovering new things different from my life. That's one of the reason I went for the exchange program. Traveling makes me relax more, think more, and absorb new energy. One of my favorite things about travel is to meet different kinds of peopl

· 70 ·

跟讀 MP3，說出令人耳目一新的自我介紹，讓面試官對你留下好印象！

2-5 面試廣播詞

✈ 面試廣播詞／機上廣播

廣播詞是國內航空公司必考的內容，中文、英文、台語的廣播詞都是常見題型。這個部分是最容易準備及拿分的，大家千萬要把握廣播詞的部分，只要在家裡做好練習，面試時輕鬆大方地唸出來通常都可以獲得不錯的印象。

✈ 面試念廣播詞注意事項

在面試時最大的敵人就是緊張，常有許多平時表現很優異的考生因為緊張而在關鍵時刻失敗了。所以最重要的是放鬆、讓心情保持在一個最平穩的狀態，才能將平常的實力展現出來。

▶▶▶ 1. 深吸一口氣

念廣播詞前先深吸一口氣，調整自己的呼吸也在這小段的時間裡讓自己冷靜下來。若是呼吸平穩了，句子唸起來會順暢許多，斷句才會有節奏。

· 108 ·

面試廣播詞考題大集錦！

3-1 艙內服務訓練-1：發送熱毛巾

Track 27

T▸ Trainee 訓練生　P▸ Pax 乘客　R▸ Trainer 訓練員

(crew giving out hot towels)　　　（空服員發送熱毛巾）

T▸ Hello, sir. Good morning. Would　訓練生▸哈囉，早安。需
you like a hot towel?　　　　　　要毛巾嗎？

P▸ What is it for?

T▸ To clean yours

R▸ Wait, wait, wai
CLEAN YOURSEL
the towels. You ca
to refresh.

T▸ Oh, yes, it is fo

空服員飛行英語日記，收錄職場實戰情境對話！

Part 3　空服員飛行英語日記

單字解析

❶ landing cards 入境卡
Foreigners require landing cards while entering another country.
外國人在入境別的國家時需要入境卡。
➢ 入境卡也可說 arrival card、entry card、custom form。

❷ transfor　v.　轉
I will transfer in H
我會先在香港轉機
➢ connecting fli

❸ get off 離開、下…
I got off the pla
city.
我大概四點的時候
➢ 下飛機也可以用

❹ require　v.　需要
All passengers
their boarding p
所有登機的乘客都

3-2｜艙內服務訓練-2：發送入境卡

❺ hold　v.　持有
I am holding an Australian passport but my origin is Taiwan.
我持著澳洲護照，但我來自台灣。
➢ 持有某國護照用 hold 這個動詞

常用短句

❶ How are you? 你好嗎？
外國人見面時最常用也一定會說的招呼語，就像是臺灣人見面時會說的最近過得怎麼樣？最近如何呀？除了 how are you 之外，也常常會聽到外國人說 How are you doing、How is it going、What's up、What have you been up to... 等等都是見面時的問候語。在登機時除了問候早安晚安之外，和乘客說一句 how are you 會顯得更親切，也能簡單開啟你們的對話！

· 139 ·

另補充單字、短句解析，上工後口說英文不出糗！

目次
Contents

Part 3 空服員飛行英語日記

Part *4* **附錄**

招考資訊

1-1 航空公司與航空聯盟簡介

中華航空空司 China Airlines

　　中華航空(China Airlines)成立於 1959 年，為台灣第一大民用航空業者並且於 2011 年加入天合聯盟成為其中會員。中華航空至今為止，共飛有 28 個國家、112 個航點，包括歐洲、美洲、大洋洲、亞洲等區域。華航的企業願景為「值得信賴，邁向卓越」，並且以用熱忱感動客戶、用關懷照顧員工、用行動支持夥伴、用文化回饋社會、用永續呵護地球以及用誠信滿足股東等六大使命著手實行，追求永續發展共生共榮的未來。

（以上資料參考華航官網。）

長榮航空 EVA Air

　　長榮航空（EVA Air）成立於 1991 年，至今飛航的航點遍佈亞洲、澳洲、歐洲及美洲等六十多個城市，並且在 2013 年成為星空聯盟的會員之一。長榮航空以飛航安全快捷、服務親切周到、經營有效創新等理念經營企業。而長榮航空最有名的 Hello Kitty 彩繪機，更成為航空業創新的行銷範例。另外，長榮航空也自 2004 年以來，數次獲得德國專業航空雜誌 Aero International 雜誌，評選為全世界十大安

全航空公司之一以及美國著名旅遊雜誌 Travel & Leisure 更於 2010 年及 2012 年評比長榮航空為「全球十大最佳航空公司（Top Ten International Airlines）」。

（以上資料參考長榮航空官網。）

國泰航空 Cathay Pacific Airways

國泰航空（Cathay Pacific Airways）創辦於 1946 年，為寰宇一家航空聯盟成員之一。國泰航空以香港為基地航行於全球，與旗下的港龍及香港華民航空於全世界運行 130 多個航點。國泰航空使命包括安全至上、培育致勝團隊、產品服務傲視同儕、貫徹發自內心的服務理念、追求理想回報、與香港攜手並進、履行環保及企業社會責任等。其歷年來多次獲得國際肯定，並且也在 2015 年獲得 JACDEC Airline Safety Ranking 2015 評選為全球最佳飛行記錄航空公司。

（以上資料參考國泰航空官網。）

新加坡航空 Singapore Airlines

新加坡航空（Singapore Airlines）成立於 1947 年，本名原為馬來西亞航空，於 1972 年分割出來，另名為新加坡航空，以新加坡為基地，至今飛行航點遍佈於六大洲。新加坡航空以創新聞名航空界，其創新的紀錄包括，第一個在經濟艙內提空免費餐飲的航空公司（1970 年代）、第一家介紹機上衛星通話系統（1991 年）、在 2007 年第一家飛行 A380 機型的航空公司等等。而新加坡航空的願景則是讓每位乘客在飛行的時候都感覺像在家一樣舒適，乘客的喜好更

是新航在發想新服務時的第一考量。

（以上資料參考新加坡航空。）

 Star Alliance 星空聯盟

　　星空聯盟（Star Alliance）是一個全球性的航空公司網絡，成立於 1997 年 5 月 14 日，為全球第一家航空公司聯盟。其總部位於德國法蘭克福，至今聯盟成員數已達 26 個，為現在歷史最悠久且規模最大的航空公司聯盟。星空聯盟的宗旨為「通過既定流程，建立管理、聯盟產品和服務的領導地位」。星空聯盟品牌也代表著，無論旅客位於世界何處，都盡力為他們提供順暢的旅行體驗。

　　星空聯盟間的合作方式為：共同的里程累積酬賓計畫、兼容優惠服務、「同一屋簷下」計畫、隨著全球網絡的建立協調一致的定期航班、單張機票可搭乘聯盟其他航空公司的航班、共用的航線網絡及停機位等等。而其聯盟下的航空公司包括，長榮航空（EVA Air）、新加坡航空（Singapore Airlines）、全日本空輸（All Nippon Airways）、韓亞航空（Asiana Airlines）、中國國際航空公司（Air Chian）等等。

（以上資料參考星空聯盟官方網站。）

Sky Team 天合聯盟

　　天合聯盟（Sky Team）為 2000 年創立的航空聯盟，初期由法國航空、達美航空、墨西哥國際航空和大韓航空聯合成立，至今已有

20 家航空公司會員，為規模第二的航空聯盟。天合聯盟的目標為提高營運效率，而其合作方式有，「同一屋簷下」計畫、依照全球網路的建立協調一致的定期航班、共同航線及停機位、推出天合優享（為第一家推出整體優惠的航空聯盟）等等。天合聯盟會員包括中華航空（China Airlines）、中國東方航空（China Eastern）、中國南方航空（China Southern）、法國航空（Air France）、達美航空（Delta Airlines）等等。

（以上資料參考天合聯盟官方網站。）

✈ One World 寰宇一家

寰宇一家（One World）為 1999 年成立的航空聯盟，為全球第三大航空聯盟，總部座落於美國紐約。目前有 15 家會員航空公司，包括國泰航空（Cathay Pacific Airways）、港龍航空（Dragonair）、美國航空（American Airlines）、英國航空（British Airways）、日本航空（Japan Airlines）等等。

寰宇一家的宗旨是成為國際飛行常客的第一個航空聯盟選擇，替乘客、合作夥伴及員工產生更多價值。其運行方式包括，讓國際旅行變得更順暢、更簡單且擁有更好的價值及回饋、提供高標準的品質、服務及安全等等。其服務範圍包含 155 個國家，並且超過千個地點。

（以上資料參考寰宇一家官方網站。）

1 招考資訊

2 100% 應試準備教戰

3 空服員飛行英語日記

4 附錄

1-2　求職廣告怎麼看

從何得知徵才消息？

　　在網路發達的現代生活，我們幾乎可以透過網路就得知徵才訊息，常見的不外乎網路上的人力銀行、該公司的官方網站上、朋友口耳相傳，不然就是隨著社群網站興起的粉絲團或部落格上面得知。得知徵才訊息不難，不過卻也很容易就忽視而錯過機會。因此，在決定報考空服員之前，就要做好長期抗戰的心理準備，不管是人力銀行網站、航空公司網站，亦或是部落客的分享都要定期瀏覽，或是訂閱接收該訊息。面試消息一旦放出來，都是有報考時間限制的，若是截止前幾天才得知消息，會忙得手忙腳亂，更糟的是有可能來不及準備。因此，在準備投考空服員之前就是將自己的天線打開，全面接收關於空服員報告的任何消息，才不會向隅。

徵才廣告內容？

　　大家常常因為航空公司放出徵才消息太興奮，就胡亂報考一通，連徵才的內容都沒有看清楚就直接跑去面試了。熟知該公司的徵才條件、目的、時間地點等等，都是報考前必須要做的，除了達到公司需求之外，也避免自己搞不清楚狀況而在面試的時候出糗最後白忙一場。接下

來要幫助大家——剖析徵才廣告中的條件，以利報考前做好完善的準備。

通常一則徵才廣告中的內容會分成幾個部分，包括徵才目的、職務以及徵才條件，徵才目的不外乎是替公司尋求具有服務熱忱的空服人員，職務則是介紹空服員的工作內容，應徵條件則是擔任空服員需具備的能力。

✈ 徵才目的

除了國內航空公司徵才訊息外，國外的航空公司徵才消息通常是以英文公布，看對徵才目的很重要，空服員一職常以 cabin crew、flight attendant、air crew 等等稱呼，不要以為空服員只是其中一項稱呼而錯失了面試的機會。除了國內公司基地在台灣之外，國外航空公司通常會在徵才標題中提到工作的 base，像是國泰航空、新加坡航空、卡達航空、阿聯酋航空等，基地分別在香港、新加坡、卡達、杜拜等等，如果不想要離開台灣工作的朋友，千萬要看清楚該公司的 base 是在哪裡，免得到時候考上，卻又不想要離開家鄉工作，真的是兩難啊！

✈ 職務

每個航空公司的職務內容要求方式不盡相同，不過都以執行飛航時機上的安全、服務乘客、具有服務熱忱等為主，除此之外有些公司也會提到應徵者能接受不同時間班表的能力、能接受工時較長等等。看清楚這些條件做好心理準備再去應徵，才不會和原本想像中光鮮亮麗的空服員工作內容有落差喔！

✈ 應徵條件

　　關於航空公司的徵才條件從身高、年齡、學歷到外語能力都有，說要求嚴格也可，說條件多也可，不過大家千萬別看到條件就卻步，這也都是因為關乎於飛安或服務品質而有這樣的條件存在的。

▶▶▶ 身高

　　關於身高要求每家航空公司不一樣，有些是摸高能摸到 208 公分，有些是 212 公分，大家不妨了解身高條件後在家裡先練習。

▶▶▶ 年齡

　　年齡也依不同公司而有異，大部份航空公司年滿 18 歲即能報考，不過還是有航空公司要求要年滿 20 歲才能應徵。

▶▶▶ 學歷

　　每家航空公司要求不同，有些只需高中畢業即可報考，有些則需要大學文憑。建議報考前看清楚條件，並且把畢業證書或是在學證明準備起來（有些公司可以讓你畢業後再加入受訓，因此可以先交在學證明，畢業後再附上畢業證書），才不會準備資料時手忙腳亂的。

▶▶▶ 外語能力

　　外語能力是幾乎每一家航空公司都有的要求，有些還很嚴格。國內的航空公司大多是規定英語能力檢定考達到某個門檻以上以證明英語能力，如果還沒有檢定考的朋友，建議在決定報考空服員的時候就同時報考英語檢定考，可以邊準備面試邊準備檢定考，在等待面試機會的時候就可以把檢定考考起來。外商公司則是全程以英語面試，並且有團體互

動面試等，建議想要考外商公司的朋友，可以開始多利用英語和朋友對話，練習習慣了，面試的時候才不會因為生疏、緊張而表達不清。

▶▶▶ 第二外語能力

英語是必須的條件，不過第二外語就沒有限制了，有些人有第二外語能力更加分。國內航空因為航線需要，也有許多航空開始招募起日韓組員，因此具備日文或韓文條件的話在國內報考時很吃香。擁有第二外語能力是加分效果，不過沒有的人也不要擔心，不會扣分，只要把英語能力調整到最佳狀態就能加很多分了！

▶▶▶ 服務業經驗

應徵前有過服務（或空服）經驗依各家航空喜好而有不同。有些公司喜歡雇用大學剛畢業的新鮮人從頭訓練起，有些則是喜歡有過一些服務（航空）業經驗的應徵者，對於服務或航空業有一定的熟悉度，在飛行時比較快上手。不過還是要說這個部分沒有絕對，因此不用害怕自己經驗不足或是已經有其他航空業的經驗。

▶▶▶ 具有服務熱忱

空服員最最基本的條件就是在高空中具有服務熱忱了，這是一個每家航空公司都想要看到的條件。想要報考的朋友不妨在應徵前想清楚自己是否具備這項條件，或者是有什麼過去的經驗能突顯自己在這方面的特性，在面試的時候可以跟面試官多聊聊這方面的經驗。

▶▶▶ 職前健康檢查

空服員是一個作息很不穩定的職業，加上工作環境是在 36000 英

呎高的機艙內，身體的適應力要很好，當然如果本來身體狀況比較不佳的人，公司可能就會考慮要不要雇用你。職前健康檢查通常是在全部的面試都通過之後，公司才會通知你進行健康檢查，檢查合格即可參加，受訓不合格只好下次再見。建議考生維持健康的作息，把身體調整到做好的狀態，除了在準備面試的過程中能有好心情之外，也好面對接下來的健康檢查以及受訓生活。

✈ 外商公司徵才廣告

▶▶▶ Cathay Pacific- Flight Attendant (Hong Kong base)

Key responsibilities:

❶ Carry out inflight safety and security procedures.

❷ Provide excellent customer service exceeding passengers expectation.

❸ Anticipate and respond to passengers needs promptly and in a professional way.

Requirements:

❶ Citizen of Taiwan

❷ Minimum age of 18

❸ High school graduated

❹ Speak and read English and Mandarin fluently. A third language is preferable.

❺ Great interpersonal skills as well as positive manner and customer-oriented.

❻ Experienced in service industry is more likely welcome.

❼ An arm-reach of 208cm and physical fitness to pass the pre-employment medical assessment

＊Male applicants should be exempted from or have completed military service.

▶▶▶ 國泰航空－空服員（基地位於香港）

職務：

❶ 實行機上安全和保安程序

❷ 提供精湛的服務品質並且超越乘客期望

❸ 專業地滿足顧客需要

應徵條件：

❶ 具中華民國國籍者

❷ 年滿 18 歲

❸ 高中畢業

❹ 具備流利英語及中文能力，第三語言尤佳

❺ 具良好的互動能力且有服務熱忱

❻ 具備服務業經驗尤佳

❼ 必須通過職前的健康檢查及 208 公分的摸高測驗

＊男性應徵者必須服完兵役或免役。

▶▶▶ Scoot Airline- Cabin Crew (based in Singapore) （參考空姐報報 Emily Post）

Responsibilities:

❶ You will travel the world when you fly with us, and you are going to have fun.

❷ You will meet new friends all over the world.

❸ You will meet passengers needs at the same time ensure the safety.

＊All with smile and Scootitude.

Requirements:

❶ Height must be or above 158cm for female and 165 cm for male.

❷ Diploma and above.

❸ Minimum age of 18.

❹ Speak fluent English.

❺ Ability of Japanese or Korean is preferable.

❻ Willing to base in Singapore.

▶▶▶ 新加坡酷航─空服員（基地位於新加坡）

職務：

❶ 加入我們你可以環遊世界

❷ 你可以結交世界各地的朋友

❸ 你會照顧乘客並同時確保飛行安全

＊具服務熱忱與酷航態度

應徵條件：

❶ 身高必須滿 158 公分（女性）或 165 公分（男性）

❷ 具高中（或以上）文憑

❸ 須年滿 18 歲

❹ 具有流利的英語能力

❺ 能說日文或韓文尤佳

❻ 能於新加坡基地工作

2 Part

100%應試準備教戰

2-1 求職信（Cover Letter）

為什麼要寫求職信？

　　求職信是一份附在履歷前面的自我推薦信，是一個非常精簡的自我介紹，也是主管透過紙本對你的第一印象。完成一份好的求職信，可以替你的整體印象加很多分。

　　求職信的目的是要讓主管透過求職信了解你應徵的動機，從龐大的應徵者信件當中脫穎而出爭取和主管面試的機會。因此，求職信表達的是你比其他人更能勝任這份工作。求職信和履歷不同的是，求職信是讓主管對你產生好的第一印象進而面試你，信中通常精簡的提到自己能夠勝任這份工作的能力、特質，履歷則是在面試之前主管可以更進一步了解你過去的學經歷和能力。

求職信裡該寫些什麼？

　　求職信大致上分成三個部分，包括抬頭（應徵者的姓名、聯絡方式）、正文（求職信的主要段落）以及結尾（署名）。

　　抬頭的部分可以選擇將段落靠左或置中，包括應徵者的姓名、聯絡方式，以及欲應徵公司的聯絡方式。收件者則是直接寫應徵主管的名字，盡量避免 Dear Sir 或 Dear who it may concerns，這是一個很粗糙的寫法，一來透露出你不熟悉該公司，二米這封信本來就是給主管看的，因此寫上其名字會感覺更親切更直接。如果真的不知道主管名字的話，可以用 Human Resource Manager 稱呼。

　　正文的部分可以分成三個段落，第一個段落 opening paragraph，說明你從何得知此職缺消息，以及清楚說明你應徵的是哪個職缺。一間公司有許多部門，有時候他們會同時發出不同部門的職缺消息，而應徵者的信件通常都是統一由人事部門收件，因此在一開頭的段落就清楚說明你是要應徵哪個職缺很重要，人事部門沒有時間一一細讀成千上萬的應徵信件，直接了當的說明此信件目的並不是貪心，而是必要的。

　　第二個段落 main paragraph 主要是說明你的個人特質及能力，這部分不必敘述的太詳細，列出幾個突出的個人特質即可，因為接下來的履歷會有更詳盡的學經歷說明。然後，這些個人特質最好是用其成就來表示，例如你有很好的領導能力，但你可以換個方式說你曾經在某個部門當過幾年的 manager 等等，這些個人特質或能力最好與你要應徵的職務有直接相關，讓主管看見你有能力勝任此職務。

　　第三個段落 closing paragraph 通常是感謝主管抽空閱讀這份求職信，並且期待能夠聽見他們的回覆。如果想要更主動得知是否有面試機會，不妨說明將會在某某時間聯絡貴公司看看是否需要提供自己更進

一步的資訊。記得確保有留下有效的聯絡方式，免得主管真的想要和你面試而聯絡不上。

　　最後是署名的部分，通常我們會在信件的結尾附上 Sincerely Yours 或者著是 Best Regards，如果是紙本印刷的話記得簽上自己的名字表示誠意，如果是電子檔的話就將自己的簽名掃描附上去。

寫求職信該注意什麼？

▶▶▶ 1.口氣堅定誠懇

　　這是一封給人事主管看的求職信，換句話說就是一封推薦自己的信，最重要的就是告訴主管你有可能是他們在找的人才，說服他們給你面試的機會。因此在信中有著堅定有自信的態度是很重要的，要讓閱讀這封信的人相信你說的話，讓人感受到你的誠懇。當然，也不要過分自信，忠實陳述自己的強項，強調自己的能力能勝任該職務。

▶▶▶ 2.內容精簡扼要

　　求職信目的是讓主管對你有初步的認識，如果希望進一步瞭解才會接著看你的履歷或者邀請你來面試，因此，求職信的內容不宜過長。要在有限制的篇幅內推銷自己，內容必定要是精華中的精華，最好是精簡扼要的說明自己應徵職務、該職務所需的能力是自己的強項、以及致謝詞等等。主管有成千上萬的求職信和自傳要看，因此太簡短或太冗長的求職信都不會吸引他們的注意的。精簡扼要地傳達自己的面試意圖即可。

▶▶▶ 3. 求職信篇幅

前面提及到，求職信只是為了吸引主管的注意力讓其進而想認識你這個人、看你的履歷、面試等，因此篇幅不宜過長，通常一張 A4 大小的頁面一頁即可，信中段落控制在三至五段，並且以 12 號的字體大小、三段為佳。

▶▶▶ 4. 照片

求職信不是履歷，因此千萬記得不要在此頁附上照片。

▶▶▶ 5. 聯絡方式

在求職信的最上方會寫上自己的地址電話等，記得再三檢查聯絡方式是否為正確或有效的，以免主管真的想要找你面試而聯絡不上你。

▶▶▶ 6. 提及該職務所需能力

在求職信中我們提及自己在哪裡看到這份職缺，而這份求職廣告中會說明應徵者需要具備怎樣的條件。因此，在求職信中我們可以精簡的說明自己和這份職務所對應的能力，讓主管在第一時間就明白你是有這方面經驗或能力的人，進而想和你面試。

▶▶▶ 7.反覆校對

　　求職信是主管對於面試者的第一且最直接的印象，在還沒有見到面試者之前就已經透過求職信幫你打分數了，因此正確且語意流暢的求職信是對閱讀者的基本禮貌也是對自己負責任的表現。然而，人們在打字的時候常常會因為外在環境而影響表達的準確度，或者是因為拼音自動校正而出現錯誤。反覆的校對十次以上，試著反覆閱讀求職信、找朋友檢查是否有不通順的地方，可以避免掉很多錯誤，才不會讓主管覺得你對這份面試不重視。

▶▶▶ 8.書寫英文時避免全部大寫

　　在求職信的最上方需要填上自己和對方的姓名住址，在信中也會因為提及自己專業技能或經驗而書寫英文，在信中要避免使用全大寫的英文（有些正式表格會要求人們填寫時使用全大寫），不過在求職信中是以清楚閱讀為主，全大寫的英文閱讀起來會比較吃力，所以不要誤會英文需要用全大寫，正常的使用大小寫即可。另外，在書寫英文的時候也避免縮寫，英文縮寫是比較快速方便的表達方式，不同領域也有不同的縮寫，因此在比較正式的求職信中請避免縮寫以免產生誤會。

▶▶▶ 9.信尾簽名、日期

在我們寫書信的時候通常會在信的最後附上自己的簽名，求職信為信件的一種，因此也需要簽上自己的名字以表示誠意。如果是用書寫的話就直接簽上自己的名字，如果是用電子郵件傳遞的話，可以將自己的簽名掃描到電腦後附在信件的最後面。另外，像書寫信件一樣，在求職信中也別忘記附上日期。

▶▶▶ 10. 求職信＝你

最後，記得求職信代表著你的一切。你的書寫能力、表達能力以及組織能力，從求職信可以看出一個人的性格及處理事情的態度，只不過是一張 A4 紙但卻能改變你的人生。所以謹慎書寫、反覆檢查、用字精確、自信卻不過分表達，將自己的專業呈現給主管，告訴他們你就是他們在尋找的人。

1 招考資訊

2 100％應試準備教戰

3 空服員飛行英語日記

4 附錄

求職信範例

▶▶▶ 範例一

Jenny Wu

No.1, Apple Rd.,

Banana City, Taiwan.

Tel | +886123456789

Email | jennywu123@email.com

1.1.2016

Mr. William Jameson

Employment Manager

Abc Corporation

13764 Street

xyz city

williamjameson@email.com

Dear Mr. Jameson,

From ABC official website, I learned about the requirement for this position. I am submitting an application for the cabin crew position of ABC airlines. I had been living in U.S.A for few years, since then I had a great interest in different cultures. Therefore, I have always wanted to become ABC's cabin crew to explore the world.

In addition to fluent English ability, I am an open minded, optimistic and cheerful person. I am a good communicator and cooperator in a team as well as helping others. According to above, I actively attend in lots of activities. In 2015, I was the translator of the International Education Expo, which helped students get more information about different colleges around the world. I was the bridge between Taiwanese student and the representatives from international colleges. Therefore, I am good at communicating as well as seeing the questions, and solving them with patience and calmness.

Last but not least, I hope I have this honor to join ABC airlines. I believe I can bring happiness on the aircraft as well as dealing with different kind of issues. Thank you for your consideration and I am looking forward to hearing from you. Within next week, I will contact you to answer any questions you may have. Thank you.

Sincerely *Jenny Wu*
（簽名）

1 招考資訊

2 100%應試準備教戰

3 空服員飛行英語日記

4 附錄

▶▶▶ 中譯

Jenny Wu

No.1, Apple Rd.,

Banana City, Taiwan.

Tel | +886123456789

Email | jennywu123@email.com

1.1.2016

Mr. William Jameson

Employment Manager

Abcde Corporation

13764 Street

xyz city

williamjameson@email.com

Dear Mr. Jameson,

我從貴公司的官網得知此份職缺,我想要應徵貴公司空服員的職缺。我曾經在美國住過幾年,自此我對於不同的文化有極大的興趣,因此,我一直以來都很想要成為貴公司的空服員去探索世界。

我除了擁有良好的英文溝通能力之外,我也是一個很開放、積極且正向的人。在團隊中我是一個很好的溝通者和合作者,我也樂於幫助他人。因此,我積極參加許多活動。在 2015 年時,我擔任國際教育展場的翻譯人員,我的工作是幫助學生了解世界各地大學的資訊,我扮演的角色

是台灣學生以及國際學校代表間的橋樑。因此，我不但是一個良好的溝通者、傾聽者，我也能夠清楚地抓住問題的重點，也能夠有耐心、冷靜地針對問題找出解決的辦法。

最後，我希望我有此榮幸擔任貴公司的空服員，我相信我能在高空中帶來歡樂，也能同時積極的處理各種問題。謝謝您的考量，我很希望能夠聽到您的消息，另外，我會在一個禮拜內聯絡您，針對您可能對我有的疑問回答。謝謝。

Sincerely　*Jenny Wu.*

（簽名）

▶▶▶ 範例二

Abby Chen

No.1, Apple Rd.,

Banana City, Taiwan.

Tel | +886123456789

Email | abbychen@email.com

12.1.2016

Mr. John Edison

Employment Manager

Abcde Corporation

13764 Street

xyz city

johnedison@email.com

Dear Mr. Edison,

I am submitting an application for the cabin crew position. This July, I just returned from two months of backpack traveling in Europe. Independent traveling through 4 different countries gives me the chance to interact and make friends with different people around the world. With the great enthusiasm in reaching new people, I believe I can do well in cabin crew position.

In 2015, I had done a one-month internship at the leading Edenspiekermann in Berlin. During that month, I worked in a multi-cultural and multi-language environment. We managed to deal with different kinds of topic everyday. In our team, I played the part of a good communicator. Being a good communicator, organizing and listening are as well important. Hence, I am an open-minded person, and willing to collect feedbacks from others, which is very important in a team.

I hope I have this pleasure to meet you and I am looking forward to hearing from you. I will contact you within a week to see if you have any queries. Thank you again for your time.

Sincerely *Abby Chen.*

（簽名）

▶▶▶ 中譯

Abby Chen

No.1, Apple Rd.,

Banana City, Taiwan.

Tel∣+886123456789

Email∣abbychen@email.com

12.1.2016

Mr. John Edison

Employment Manager

Abcde Corporation

13764 Street

xyz city

johnedison@email.com

Dear Mr. Edison,

我想要應徵我在貴公司官網上看到有關空服員的職缺。這個七月，我獨自一個人前往歐洲實行兩個月的背包客旅行，找到了四個不同的國家，也因為這次背包客旅行的經驗，讓我有機會可以和不同國籍的人互動以及交朋友。懷抱著對於與人們交流的熱情，我相信我可以勝任空服員的這份職位。

2015 年，我在柏林的 Edenspiekermann 實習了一個月。我們實習的地方是一個多國家且多語言的環境，我們每天都要處理、討論不同的議

題，並且找出解決的方法。在團隊中，我是一個好的溝通者，當然，好的溝通者也包含著良好的組織以及聆聽能力，因此，我是一個開放、並且很能夠接受別人意見的人。而這些能力都是在一個團隊中不可或缺的因素。

希望我有這個機會可以見到您，也很期待可以從您那邊聽到消息。我會在一個禮拜內聯絡您，看看是否有任何問題我可以回答的。再次謝謝您撥冗看我的履歷。

Sincerely　*Abby Chen*

（簽名）

2-2 履歷（Resume）

在簡單地介紹完自己之後，如果主管有興趣認識你接著就會看你的履歷。我們常聽到的履歷有兩種稱法，一是履歷 CV（Curriculum Vitae）和簡歷 Resume，若是公司沒有特別要求，一般我們交的是履歷 Resume，CV 比起 Resume 較多用在申請學位時遞交的履歷。

✈ CV 和 Resume 的差異？

Resume 是你的技能、經驗和教育的總結，通常為一頁不超過兩頁，履歷的筆調是很簡潔並且精確的，如果你有太多的學經歷、活動經驗，那麼就盡量放與你應徵職位有相關的經歷。既然叫做簡歷，不會有人想要看你歷年來做過全部的大大小小的事情或成就，挑幾個重要的來寫即可。

Curriculum Vatae 源自於拉丁文，指的是一個人一生以來做過了哪些事情。因此它是一個涵蓋個人更多細節的履歷，包括一個人的教育程度、學術成就、工作背景、研究經驗，以及其他獎項等等，CV 大部份是用來申請更高階的學位，也因為如此 CV 也可以稱為是 acadamic resume—學術上的履歷。

在歐洲、中東、非洲或亞洲，大部份的主管對 CV 和 Resume 沒

有特定的要求，通常指的就是簡歷，對 CV 和 Resume 有明顯的要求主要是在美國，在美國 CV 主要是用來申請學術、教育或研究等的職位，也可申請獎學金。因此在台灣的話，應徵工作主要還是以簡歷為主。

怎麼寫履歷？

履歷主要是以一頁 A4 大小的紙清楚概要的方式陳列出你的學經歷和個人特質，其中包括你的個人資料、專長、學歷、經驗、技能、特殊成就等等，可以依照個人學經歷或職位需求等擺放不同成就或技能。除了掌握上述在討論求職信的書寫原則之外（包括口氣堅定誠懇、內容精簡扼要、聯絡方式、反覆校對、避免全部大寫等等），在大家都擁有不同學經歷的條件下，如何能脫穎而出讓主管雇用你，以下幾個要點要特別注意：

▶▶▶ 1.履歷長度

履歷的長度盡量以一頁為原則，最多不超過兩頁。不要因為想要告訴老闆你得過多少獎、參加過多少活動就把所有事蹟都放在履歷裡面，挑重要的或是與應徵工作最相關的資訊來講就夠了，不然主管可能在閱讀你的履歷的時候因為太多內容而忽略你真正想要表達的重點。

▶▶▶ 2.排版

履歷的字體通常為 10-12，盡量統一用同一個大小的字體，不要隨便更換字型也不要因為強調個人風格而採用可愛、藝術風格的字型，閱讀起來舒服是最重要的原則。仔細想想，主管有上千份履歷要閱讀，如果連認識你都很吃力的話，他絕對不會想要繼續閱讀你的履歷。把握

一個原則，排版以整齊乾淨為主。

▶▶▶ 3. 時間排序

寫履歷的時候，時間的排序是以比較近期開始往前寫。因為求職者眾多加上通常選才的時間有限，一般在閱讀履歷時只會從每個大標下挑幾個重點看，因此放在前面的學經歷會最先被閱讀到，如果以順序法從古時代的事蹟開始寫，主管可能就會忽略到你最新的近況。最重要的是，在每一項學經歷都要附上日期。

▶▶▶ 4. 避免空泛的詞彙

人們在寫履歷時常犯的一個錯誤就是在描述自己的能力或特質的時候，使用過多空泛的詞彙，而空泛的詞彙常常讓人不知道你的能力程度到哪裡。比方說你想表達你的英文程度很好，I am good at English 是絕對表達不出你的英文程度的，英文程度有多好？怎樣子的好？都要具體的寫出來，像是 I speak fluent English 或是附上具體的檢定成績。又或是想表達自己在團隊中扮演一個很好的角色，I am good at working in a team 這樣是看不出你在團隊中的角色的，具體的說出自己是 supportive, cooperative, detailed-thinker or adaptable 等等，可以幫助說明你在團隊中的角色。記得，空泛華麗的詞彙是沒辦法包裝你的能力的。

▶▶▶ 5. 敘述方式

以條列式取代文章式的方法敘述。將自己的學經歷、能力以條列式的方式陳述，而非用像說故事的方式寫成一段一段的段落，如此一來才能幫助主管閱讀，加速對你的認識。

▶▶▶ 6.客製化你的履歷

　　我們在應徵工作的時候絕對不會是只應徵一家公司而已，但有許多人以「一式多投」的方式在投遞履歷，這樣並不會幫助你得到工作機會，也有可能因為寫得太「多功能」而忽略了各家公司所要求的條件。因此，客製化你的履歷，針對各家公司的企業文化、所要求的條件著手，才能幫助你的履歷脫穎而出。

▶▶▶ 7.避免使用「我」、「我們」

　　在寫履歷的時候避免使用第一人稱亦或第三人稱，每個句子以動詞作為開頭。例如避免 I managed the customer service website. 而是以 Managed the customer service website. 表達。

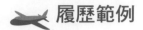 履歷範例

▶▶▶ 範例一

Jessica Lin

PERSONAL DATA

Date of Birth | 01 January, 1990

Tel | +886123456789

Address | No.1, Apple Rd., Banana Township, Orange County, Taiwan.

Email | jessicalin@email.com

HIGHLIGHTS OF QUALIFICATIONS

❑Excellent English ability of speaking, listening, writing, and reading. Capable of communicating with foreigners.

❑A good team player and quick learner. Work easily and confidently.

❑Great enthusiasm in helping and serving others.

❑Great problem-solving skills and positive attitude.

EDUCATION

September 2009-June 2012

National University of Kaohsiung

Bachelor of Arts.　　Major: English　　Minor: Japanese

September 2006-June 2009

National Kaohsiung Senior High School

WORK EXPERIENCES

February 2014-April, 2014

Case assistant of Center for Education Research and Evaluation, National Taiwan Normal University.

October 2009-June 2012

Assistant of Engineering College, National University of Kaohsiung.

October 2009-December 2009

English Tutor of elementary school student.

ACTIVITIES

2012

The student member of the 2012 International Academic Competence workshop.

2011

Interpreter of 2011 Spring International Education Expo.

The main role and the art leader of 9th Graduation Play of Department of Western Languages and Literature, National University of Kaohsiung.

2009-2010

The chief of activities of student association, Department of Western Languages and Literature, National University of

Kaohsiung.

SKILLS

English | Fluent

TOEIC | 885/990 (30 March, 2014)

GEPT | Intermediate (30 March, 2008)

Mandarin | Excellent

Taiwanese | Well

▶▶▶ 中譯

Jessica Lin

個人資料

姓名 | Jessica, Lin

生日 | 01 January, 1990

電話 | +886123456789

地址 | No.1, Apple Rd., Banana Township, Orange County, Taiwan.

Email | jessicalin@email.com

能力

❑良好的聽說讀寫英語能力，能與外國人溝通

❑好的團隊夥伴，學習快速，工作輕鬆有自信

❑對於幫助別人有極大的熱情

❑能積極、冷靜地處理問題

學歷

2009 9 月-2012 6 月

國立高雄大學 西洋語文學系

2006 9 月-2009 6 月

國立高雄中學

工作經歷

2014 2 月-2014 4 月

國立台灣師範大學教育評鑑中心行政助理

2009 10 月-2012 6 月

國立高雄大學工學院助理

2009 10 月-2009 12 月

國小英語家教

活動

2012

2012 International Academic Competence workshop 學員

2011

2011 春季國際教育展口譯人員

國立高雄大學第九屆西洋語文學系畢業公演女主角

2009-2010

國立高雄大學西洋語文學系活動部長

技能

英語 | 聽說讀寫流利（多益：885 / 990、全民英檢中級）

中文｜聽說讀寫流利

台語｜聽說流利

▶▶▶ 範例二

Kelly Lee

Phone_　+886123456789

Email_　kellylee@email.com

Address_ No.1, Apple Rd., Banana Township, Orange

County, Taiwan.

Personal Qualification

A quick learner, positive thinking, and proactive person.

Expe rience

10.2014-09.2015

Ground staff of Far East Airlines

07.2013-09.2014

Summer volunteer intern of Cathay Pacific Airlines

10.2011-07.2013

Stewardess of 85c cafe

Educati on

09.2010-06.2014

Wenzao Ursuline University of Languages
Department of Japanese
09.2007-06.2010
Taichung High School

Activities

2015 Volunteer Japanese translator of Japanese Culture
Academic Affairs
2015 Chief of Manga association of Wenzao Ursuline
University
2014 Volunteer of animal protect affair

Skills

English_Fluent
TOIEC_950/990 (05.2014)
GEPT_High level (02.2013)
Japanese_Fluent
JLPT_N2
Mandarine_Fluent
Native speaker
Taiwanese_Fluent
Native speaker

▶▶▶ 中譯

Kelly Lee

Phone_　+886123456789

Email_　kellylee@email.com

Address_ No.1, Apple Rd., Banana Township, Orange County, Taiwan.

關於我

快速學習者、正向思考、主動積極

工作經驗

10.2014-09.2015

遠東航空公司地勤人員

07.2013-09.2014

國泰航空公司暑期實習生

10.2011-07.2013

85 度 c 服務生

教育程度

09.2010-06.2014

文藻外語大學日本語學系

09.2007-06.2010

國立台中高中

活動經歷

2015 日本學術文化交流會翻譯員

2015 文藻大學漫畫社社長

2014 動物保護運動義工

語言能力

英文__流利

多益 _950/990 （05.2014）

全民英檢 _ 高級（02.2013）

日語__流利

日文檢定__N2

中文__流利（母語）

台語__流利（母語）

▶▶▶ 範例三

Amy Huang

Date of Birth | 01 January, 1992

Tel: +886123454321

Address | No.1, Apple Rd., Banana Township,

Orange County, Taiwan.

Email | amyhuang@email.com

Professional Qualities

Troubleshooter, good solving problems skills

A good team player, cooperative and supportive

Keen insight into customers' needs

See what needs doing without being told

Education

09.2011-present

Tamkang University, Department of Communication

09.2008-06.2011

Taoyuan National High School

Work Experiences

05.2011-05.2012

TVBS News Department Producing Assistant

Assisting the process of shows

2010.10-05.2011

Journalist of CCTV

Collecting and reporting news

Activities

09.2014-05.2015

Member of Tamkang University Debating club

04.2012-05.2015

Member of Tamkang University guitar club

Skills

English | Fluent

GEPT | Intermediate (30 March, 2012)

Mandarin | Excellent

▶▶▶ 中譯

Amy Huang

Date of Birth | 01 January, 1992
Tel | +886123454321
Address | No.1, Apple Rd., Banana Township,
Orange County, Taiwan.
Email | amyhuang@email.com

個人能力

問題解決者，擁有處理問題的好能力
好的團隊夥伴，扮演合作並且支持的角色
瞭解顧客的需求
主動行動而非被告知行動

教育程度

09.2011-現在
淡江大學大傳學系
09.2008-06.2011
桃園高中

工作經驗

05.2011-05.2012
TVBS 新聞部製作助理

協助節目製作流程

2010.10-05.2011

CCTV 記者

收集及播報新聞

活動經歷

09.2014-05.2015

淡江大學辯論社社員

04.2012-05.2015

淡江大學吉他社社員

語言能力

英語｜流利

全民英檢｜中級 (30.03, 2012)

中文｜流利母語

2-3　自傳（Autobiography）

在空服員徵才中通常不太需要繳交自傳，頂多是履歷跟求職信而已，不過也可能因為不同航空公司有不同的要求，因此在求職之前最好把這三樣東西一起準備起來，以備不時之需。

為什麼需要自傳？

求職信的準備是為了讓主管有興趣繼續閱讀你的履歷，履歷是將你的學經歷或成就以條列式的方式展現出來，如果主管在面試之前對你還有好奇心會接著看你的自傳（如果有要求的話）。比起生硬的履歷，自傳更能展現出個人特色，也更能表達你想要告訴主管什麼，當然還是要以你應徵的職位有相關聯。

自傳怎麼寫？

一般來說自傳的長度維持在 600-800 字，並以三段來陳述，如果不需要交代太多細節，通常維持在一頁就夠了。自傳書寫的模式比較自由，並沒有硬性規定要寫什麼樣的內容，主要是依照個人想要 focus 在自己哪部分的能力或經歷，不過若是沒有頭緒，通常自傳會分成三段書寫，而每段內容如下：自傳中第一段，通常擺放自己的成長背景，不過這部分簡單帶過就好不必贅述，並且盡量與自己的人格特質做連接，

例如小時候生長在怎麼樣的家庭因此造就了自己擁有什麼樣的特質等等，要特別注意的是自己的人格特質也要和所應徵的職缺有所關連。

第二段描述自己的能力、興趣、專長等，這部分是自傳的重點，可以把與這份職缺最有關聯、最有影響性的學歷或經歷放在這一段說明，並且強調因為這份經歷自己從而獲得或是自己在某方面有很強的能力，比如說曾經在某公司的公關部門任內組織了一場大型活動，並且負責此活動所有媒體聯繫，由此可知你具有非常強的組織能力及公關技能等。不過要特別小心的是，如果與這份職缺無關的經歷就可以不必提及，例如如果你是要應徵服務相關的職缺，就也不必強調自己的文書處理能力有多強。

第三段著手在自己未來的願景潛力等，這部分可以簡單闡述你對自己未來計畫的方向，或是自己的能力可以為公司帶來什麼幫助。這部分用比較穩健的說法帶過即可，不必誇大說詞自己能為公司帶來更宏偉的未來等，這樣只會顯得自己不夠誠懇。

要特別注意的細節

▶▶▶ 1. 自傳格式

和前面提及的求職信和履歷一樣，自傳的字體和字級控制在 10-12，並且以簡單易懂的字體為主，篇幅則是以一頁為主，除非想要表達的東西真的非常重要會攸關到是否得到這次面試機會，不然盡量避免落落長的篇幅。

▶▶▶ 2.不要主動提及自己的缺點

自傳跟履歷一樣，和職缺不相關的東西就不要提及，但因為自傳的格式較不拘束，所以會讓人不小心就聊開了，比如說出現類似雖然我某某方面能力不是很厲害，但是我能夠怎樣怎樣。這樣的表達方式會讓主管認為你是個能力不足的人，如果你想表達你哪方面能力很強，就直接切入重點。

▶▶▶ 3.避免流水帳式的自傳

在寫自傳的時候人們很常犯的一個錯誤就是將自己的事蹟從頭寫到尾，很像在寫人生自傳。但記住這是一份求職的自傳，主管不會對你從幼稚園開始到現在參加了什麼活動獲得過什麼獎而感到興趣，也不會因為你參加朗讀比賽得獎而對你加分。因此挑對的、最有相關的、最能表現自己能力的事情來寫才能幫自己加分。

▶▶▶ 4.多找朋友閱讀自己的自傳

自己閱讀自己的筆調比較沒辦法找出自己的語病，多請朋友閱讀自己的自傳才能找出不通順的地方或是盲點，也可同時校正文中的錯字或語法。

▶▶▶ 5.避免套用現成格式

現在網路上有很多現成的自傳範本，雖然自傳的內容都大同小異（成長背景、經歷、未來展望等），但是面試主管每天看這麼多人的自傳，絕對可以看出這份自傳是否套用範例格式。用自己的筆調寫自傳也是表達自己個性的一種方式，所以避免套用現成的格式才不會讓主管覺得你不夠誠意。

▶▶▶ 6.與應徵職位連結

　　自傳的內容應該和你要應徵的職位做連結，不管是提到自己的生長背景、個性、能力、活動經歷、學歷等等，都要表現出和這份職位息息相關，如果不相關的就不用提及，因為主管想要了解的是你是否能夠勝任此份職務，對於其他無關的資訊其實不會幫助你得到面試的機會，反而可能因為加了這些資訊讓文章變得落落長，而讓主管忽略你真正想要表達的重點。

▶▶▶ 7.具體化自己的能力

　　如果你的英語能力很好，有多好？是在於聽說讀寫哪個方面？都要具體的表達出來，否則人人都可以說自己的英文能力很好，但到底是好到什麼程度？要有具體的實例主管才能夠瞭解。比如舉出實例說你曾經當過教育展場的翻譯或曾經是何種層級的英語老師等，這樣才能讓主管清楚了解你的英語能力程度到哪裡。

▶▶▶ 8.表達自己對面試的期望

　　在自傳的最後可以禮貌誠懇的表達自己對此次面試的盼望，讓主管了解你對這次面試機會的重視和期待。

 自傳範例

▶▶▶ 範例一

I am Ann. Due to my father's job, my family and I moved to U.S.A for few years. Growing under American culture, not only do I have a good command of English, but I also have an open-minded, optimistic and friendly personality. I like to help others and enjoy the happiness from it.

I have a great interest in attending team activities. During my college, I had been the chief of activities of student association of our department. On the other hand, I was also the main actor in our senior year graduation play. In these activities, I learned how to help others, how to communicate and cooperate in a team. As well as having experiences in part-time job such as assistant of department, waitress in cafe, I am familiar with service industry.

During college, I used to be the interpreter of the International Education Expo. I helped Taiwanese students to get to know the information of international colleges. I was the bridge between the representatives and students. Hence, I am good at listening to others and finding out others' needs. In addition, I had attended the English exchange program held by two universities. During this program, not only did I make progress of English, but I also made friends with people from different backgrounds, including science, biology, medicine, and literature. Therefore, overtime we had a topic to discuss. We exchanged very different opinions. With this experience, I learned to keep an open-minded attitude because having different opinions is a very normal thing. Everyone has their own backgrounds and stories. This is how a team and a world works, accepting diversities.

I hope I have this chance to join you. In the future, I will focus on customer service. Listening to customer's needs is my main point in this job. Thank you for reading my autobiography. I am looking forward to hearing from you. Thank you.

▶▶▶ 中譯

我是 Ann，因為爸爸工作的關係，全家曾搬去美國住幾年，在美式文化的薰陶下，除了有良好的英語能力，也造就我樂觀、友善，積極的個性。我喜歡幫助人，也能從中得到許多滿足。

我熱衷於參加團體活動，在大學期間我曾是系上的活動部長，此外，也擔任了系上畢業公演的主角。在各種團隊活動中，我累積了互相幫助、合作以及良好的溝通能力，並且透過各種打工經驗，包括家教、大學院級助理、咖啡店服務生等，充分了解服務業這個行業。

在大學期間，我曾經擔任國際教育展覽的口譯人員，口譯人員主要的工作是協助台灣學生了解如何赴國際學校唸書，在國際學校代表和台灣學生間當溝通橋樑。因此，我善於傾聽別人，並了解別人的需求。另外，我也曾經參與兩大學校合辦的英語交流菁英班。在這段期間，除了加深了英語能力之外，也結交了各種不同領域和背景的朋友，從科學、生物、醫學和文學等等背景的學生都有。也因此，在每次交流討論的時候，都能夠有來自不同背景的意見，由此活動經驗，我學習到在一個團隊中保持一個開放的態度，因為有不同的意見是一件很正常的事，每個人都有自己的背景與故事，而世界與團體之所以運作順利就在，接受多樣性。

希望我能有這個榮幸加入貴公司，在未來我會朝著顧客服務方面做努力，傾聽顧客需求。謝謝您撥冗閱讀我的自傳，希望近期內可以見到您。謝謝。

▶▶▶ 範例二

I am Lena, a positive and thoughtful person. I was born in Japan, lived there for few years and then my family and I went back to Taiwan. With Japanese descent, I am able to speak Japanese and Mandarin.

I used to major in English during college. I studied not only English literatures but also business English. As a result, I can also speak fluently English.

I have a great sense in customer industry. During college, I had been working as a part-time in a coffee shop. Not only because I love coffee, I also like to meet different people. With this job, I meet people of different backgrounds. I like to talk to them, knowing their stories. Working in a coffee shop helps me to see customers' needs in advance and to deal with various kinds of situation, such as customer complaint.

After graduating from college, I worked as a ground staff for Eva Airline. I learned a lot from this job including how to face different passengers, how to deal with various kinds of issues, how to be a good team member among colleagues. I am a quick learner who can learn new methods, new skills at any time. I am also open to new ideas. I don't judge before knowing what exactly happened. In my opinion, this is a good way to face customers. Every customer has a different situation, so no judging and putting my own self into their shoes is one of the best way to help to solve the problem.

In the future, I hope I can transfer into cabin crew. Not only because I love to travel, enjoy different cultures, but also because love to do passengers big favors. I believe I can bring happiness on board with my great ability of Japanese, English, and with my enthusiasm of helping others. Hope I have the chance to meet you in person. Thank you so much for consideration.

▶▶▶ 中譯

我是 Lena，一個積極而且貼心的人。我出生在日本，在那邊生活了幾年然後和家人一起搬回了台灣。因為有日本的血統，我可以講流利的日文跟中文。

在大學的時候我主修英文，包括英文文學還有應用商業英文，因此我也能夠說流利的英文。

我對於服務業有一定程度的瞭解。在大學期間我也在咖啡店打工，不只是因為我喜歡喝咖啡，我也喜歡認識不同的人們。這份工作讓我認識了很多來自不同背景的人，我喜歡和他們聊天、聽他們的故事。在咖啡店打工也幫助我在還沒被要求前就了解顧客的需求，也累積了處理各種狀況的能力，包括顧客投訴。

大學畢業之後我擔任長榮航空的地勤人員，這份工作讓我學到怎麼面對不同情緒的乘客，如何處理不同的事件，也讓我學到如何在團隊中扮演一個好夥伴。我是一個學習很快速的人，我隨時能學習新的方法、新的技能，對於任何新的方式我都保持著開放的態度，在還沒了解實際上發生什麼事之前，我不會隨便下斷論，對我來說，這是面對乘客的好方法，因為每個乘客都有不同的狀況，先入為主的判斷事情因果並不會帶來任何改善。因此，我試著每次都用乘客的角度去面對問題，這樣才是幫助他們最好的方法。

在未來，我希望可以轉成空服員，不只是因為我喜歡旅遊，享受接觸不同的文化，我也喜歡幫助處理乘客的事情。我相信以我的英語、日文還有我對飛行的熱誠，我可以在飛機上帶來歡樂。希望我有這個機會可以見到您，謝謝您撥冗閱讀我的自傳。

（以上範本純屬虛構，僅供參考。）

1 招考資訊

2 100%應試準備教戰

3 空服員飛行英語日記

4 附錄

自我介紹 1

Track 01

Hello everyone. I'm Lisa from Taiwan. I am a student majoring in English and minoring in Spanish as well. I once lived in Sydney, Australia as an exchange student for a year. In Sydney, I made a lot of friends coming from different countries. There were Chinese, Japanese, English, Portuguese, and so on. It is so interesting when all different nationalities meet. We shared various opinions, jokes, foods, living ways and much more. I really enjoy the life there. One thing I'd learnt during the exchange program is that the world is so much more colorful with all different kinds of culture.

I love to travel while at the same time discovering new things different from my life. That's one of the reason I went for the exchange program. Traveling makes me relax more, think more, and absorb new energy. One of my favorite things about travel is to meet different kinds of people, know their story and life. I am a positive person. I would like to live at the moment, try my best instead of regretting afterwards.

These things make me so much more passionate about being a flight attendant. I'd love to meet passengers with different nationalities, various backgrounds of crews, and also every destination I can reach to. Not only being in the destination makes me know different culture, but also the passengers on board. I believe my passion about this job can help a lot on board. Thank you.

▶▶▶ 中譯

嗨，大家好！我是麗莎，來自台灣。我現在還在唸大學，主修英文，副修西班牙文。過去我曾經在澳洲雪梨當了一年的交換學生，在那邊我認識了很多不同國家的朋友，他們有的來自中國、日本、英國、葡萄牙等等。我發現當不同國籍的人們聚在一起的時候會發生很多有趣的事情。我們有不同的意見、不一樣的玩笑、不同的食物和生活方式。我很享受在雪梨交換的日子，其中一個在這段時間學到的事情是，這個世界正是因為有這麼多不一樣的文化而擁有很多色彩。

我喜歡旅行，喜歡旅途中發現和自己生活很不一樣的新鮮事。這也是我去雪梨交換的其中一個原因。旅行能讓我放鬆、思考更多的事，並吸收正面能量。其中一個我喜歡旅行的原因是，認識不同的人們，知道他們的生活和故事。我是一個很正向的人，我喜歡活在當下，盡全力生活而不是之後再來後悔。

上述總總原因讓我對空服員充滿了熱忱和想像。我很希望遇到不同國籍的乘客、不同背景的同事，還有每一個我能飛去的城市。不只是身在不同城市時才能讓我體會不同文化，在飛機上的乘客也能讓我聽到很不一樣的故事。我相信我對於這份工作的熱忱可以在高空中帶來許多幫助！謝謝。

✈ 重點解析

❶ 在第一段開頭，以一般性的招呼語 hello 作為開場亦可換成更有時間性的打招呼方式，例如 good morning, good afternoon 等等。時間性的招呼語會讓人覺得更親切或有朝氣，不過並不是一種必要，有些人習慣以口語的 hello 作為問候也不失禮貌。另外，在介紹自己的名字時，除了可以簡單的直說 I'm Lisa 之外，有些人也喜歡以比較正式的方式介紹自己，如 my name is Lisa。在這邊沒有提及年齡因為文中提到自己是大學生，如果讀者想要提及年齡表示自己已有其他工作經驗，也可以簡單說明 I'm 24 即可。

❷ 在自我介紹中常常提及自己的興趣。文中第二段說明 I love to travel 亦是表達自己嗜好的一種方式，如果以 my hobby is... 敘述也可以，不過要小心當文中太多 my A is B 的時候，難免會讓人覺得太拘束，像是在背自我介紹稿，建議可以穿插著不同句型使用，不會太拘束又能完整表達自己。

❸ 文中以 positive 一詞描述自己的個性，除了 positive 之外，還能以 think of the bright side, optimistic, hopeful 等詞彙替代。這

些都是正面的詞彙，不過意思上還是有些許差異。positive 是指在思考某事情時，能以積極的態度面對；optimistic 則是概括的說明這個人很樂觀；hopeful 則比較是對未來或是事情抱著希望的，think of the bright side 則跟 positive 有點相像，思考時總會想到正向的一面。因此，在使用這些詞彙的時候，最好後面接著說明為何如此，才更有說服力。

❹ I love to travel at the same time discovering new things different from my life.（我喜歡旅行，同時發現和自己生活中很不一樣的新鮮事。）

在這邊用 at the same time 而不是 when，同時表達自己的嗜好及其帶來的快樂。如果以 when 表示成 I love to travel when discovering new things different from my life. 意思就會變成我在發現新鮮事的時候喜歡旅行，文意不通。若是顛倒過來 I love to discover new things different from my life when traveling. 就無法表達 travel 為興趣了。因此，若想要一次闡述兩種意思的話，可以適時地使用 at the same time instead of when。

❺ Not only... but (also)... 不只是…也是…

是一個很好用且常派上用場的句型。在敘述不只一件事情時可以避免以 and 連接，文中不可能不出現 and 不然就是出現太多次，加入不同的句型變化可以讓整個自我介紹不那麼單調。Not only being in the destination makes me know different culture, but also the passengers on board. 聽起來比 Being in the destination and the passengers make me know different culture. 順暢許多。

🛫 自我介紹 2

 Track 02

Good morning, I'm Robert, 26 years old, working as an interpreter now. I can speak fluent Mandarin, Japanese, English and also French. I work as an interpreter in a business company and also as a part-time exhibition translator. I often go on business trips abroad with my manager. Sometimes the meetings are full of business men who come from different countries. Sometimes just my manager and I are the ones. My job is to interpret reports into Japanese, English, or sometimes French from Mandarin, or the other way around. Language is my strength and hobby as well. I would love to learn different languages at any time.

I am very proactive and punctual as well. I make myself familiar with the report every time before being asked. If there is an unfamiliar topic to me, I will do research to find out the original meaning. On the other hand, I am also an easy-going person. I get along well with all of my colleagues. To me, nothing is such a big deal. I won't let small things bother me. You can choose to be cheerful for a day. I tell myself. Therefore, if there is a challenge for me, I will face it, accept it and conquer it.

In my working environment, I see lots of people speaking different kinds of languages. Though it does really intrigue me, the most interesting part is the way they express themselves. No matter which language they are speaking, facial expressions and body languages are always there, and these things will never lie. I like to observe people while they are talking. Now, I can easily understand people's moods without understanding their language.

I am not only good at interpreting in several languages but also good at being in a multi-language environment. Hence, I have the ability to understand people before they fully express themselves. I believe this will make a big difference for the passengers above 35,000 ft. Thank you.

▶▶▶ 中譯

早安，我是羅伯特，26 歲，現任口譯。我能流利地說中文、日文、英文以及法文。我任職於商業公司的口譯，也偶爾接一些展覽的翻譯工作。我經常跟著公司經理出國開會，有時國外會議參加的人們都來自不同國家，有時只有我們兩個是外國人。我的工作是將報告從中文翻譯成日文、英文或法文，或將它們翻成中文。語言是我的強項也是我的興趣，我喜歡在任何時候都能學習不同語言。

我是一個積極而且守時的人，在會議報告之前，我會熟悉報告內容，如果是比較陌生的主題，我會先做研究了解報告的原意。另外，我是一個

很好相處的人，我和同事處得很好。對我來說，沒有什麼事情是大不了的，自己才可以選擇左右一天的開心。我是這麼告訴自己。因此，如果生活上遇到什麼挑戰，我會面對接受，然後克服它。

在我的工作環境裡，我接觸到許多講不同語言的人，這真的很夢幻。不過最有趣的部分是，不管他們講的是什麼語言，一定都會伴隨著臉部表情跟肢體語言，這個部分是不會騙人的。我喜歡觀察他們的臉部和肢體語言。現在就算我不瞭解他人的語言，我也可以察覺他們的心情。

我不只擅於翻譯，也很能適應多語言的環境。因此，在別人開口說話之前，我有能力判斷他人的情緒。我相信這項技能可以在 35000 英尺高的天空中帶來一些幫助。謝謝。

重點解析

❶ 在自我介紹中，人們通常會提及自己的工作。文中以 work as... 說明自己的職務，另外也可以 my job is...、I work in...、I am a... 等等，這些詞彙都可以互相替代，皆指自己現任的工作為何。

❷ 在自我介紹中，人們常滔滔不絕想要把自己好的一面一次全部說出來，不過往往也忽略，一口氣把自己的事蹟全部講完，會讓聽者聽得很煩悶。因此，在文句中適當地穿插轉折詞，或是停頓一下，會讓人聽起來舒服許多。如第二段中 on the other hand，講完自己其中之一的個性之後，可以加個轉折詞「另外」，「另外，我也是個隨和的人」，如果在表達完自己是個積極的人之後直接又接著，

「我是一個隨和的人」，難免顯得乏味。不妨可以試著在文句中穿插一些轉折詞，讓聽者休息一下，也讓自己喘一口氣。

❸ "Though it does really intrigue me, the most interesting part is the way they express. "

"Though..., ..."（雖然…，但是…。）的句型很常被使用到，在這邊要特別注意，在此句型中很常犯的錯就是在第二個句子前加上 but，"though...but..." 是錯誤的句型，大家在使用的時候要特別小心，不要把它直接中翻英了。

❹ be good at sth. 擅長於…

在自介中經常提及自己的專長，此句型就可以派上用場。除此之外也可以以 "be skilled in sth." 替代，唯一點不同的是，"be skilled in sth" 指的比較是特別專精於某項技能，如：I am skilled in fixing electronic devices.（我善於維修電器用品。）

✈ 自我介紹 3

 Track 03

Hello everyone, I am Abby, 22 years old. I like to travel. I just came back from three months of backpacking in Europe. I traveled through three countries: Germany, Switzerland, and Italy. I love meeting different kinds of people and that's the reason I went backpacking. On the other hand, I feel traveling alone is very challenging and amazing at the same time. The amazing part of traveling is getting to meet new friends and developing new ways of thinking.

Something I learned from backpacking is that life is a maze, but you will always find a way out. Meanwhile, the process of finding the way is much more interesting and important than the exit itself. The people you meet, the culture you are engaged with and so on. They are so different but at the same time add color to it.

Traveling somehow shapes my personality. I am a positive, adventuresome and outgoing person who always like to try new stuff. I would like to know different people, hear their stories, and try different foods. I think there are so many possibilities in life. Everything is worth trying. And now I'm here, giving myself a chance to move on to my next colorful page of life as well. I hope my enthusiasm will bring a lot of joy on board, and help spread it all over the world! Thank you.

▶▶▶ **中譯**

大家好，我是艾比，今年 22 歲。我喜歡旅行，我才剛從歐洲回來完成三個月的背包客旅行。我去了德國、瑞士以及義大利三個國家。當背包客的原因之一是因為我喜歡結交不同背景的朋友。另一方面，我覺得獨自旅行是很美好，但同時卻很有挑戰性的一件事。旅行很棒的部分是認識新朋友與產生新領悟。

在當背包客時我體悟到，生命就是一場迷宮，但你永遠找得到你自己的一條路出去。而同時呢，在尋找路途的過程遠比出口本身重要且有趣的多。在路上遇到的人、你融入的文化，都是如此不一樣卻同時帶給世界不同美好的色彩。

旅行也成就我的個性。我是一個正面、喜歡冒險且外向的人，我喜歡嘗試新鮮事。我喜歡結交新朋友、了解他們的故事、品嚐不同食物等等。我認為生命有很多不同可能，而它們都值得你去嘗試。現在我站在這邊，也給我自己一個機會打開我人生的下一頁。希望我的熱情可以在空中帶來很多歡樂，並且散播到全世界！謝謝。

✈ 重點解析

❶ the reason for / why... …的原因

在自我介紹中提及自己的經歷很常需要說明為什麼這麼做之類，因此做某件事的原因可以用 the reason for / why... 來表述，很實用又很清楚。

❷ learn from... 從…學到

這個片語也很實用，在自我介紹中可以拿來用，在提及自己過去工作經歷或活動經驗的時候，可以順便說明自己學到了什麼。除了讓面試官知道你有這樣的經歷之外，將自己學到、體會到的東西分享給他們，也會讓面試官覺得你能夠在處理事情中學習成長喔。

❸ outgoing 外向的

在文中表示自己外向的 outgoing 也可以以 extrovert 一詞表達。

❹ meanwhile 同時

在自我介紹的時候，常常會太積極想要介紹自己同時把很多形容詞或句子連接在一起，中間只用一個 and…and…連貫下去。meanwhile 是一個很好用的連接詞，除了可以連接兩個形容詞，也可以連接兩個句字。

✈ 自我介紹 4

 Track 04

Good morning everyone. It's Kate from Malaysia. I once worked for China Airlines as a member of the ground staff for 2 years. I can speak Malay, Mandarin and English as well. Despite the fact that aviation affairs were the main job, communicating with passengers was also the most important part of it. Hence I am a reliable, flexible, and positive person. Passengers sometimes overreacted when some travel issues were not settled. In addition to apologizing to them, I tried my best to figure out how to arrange things for them. After my suggestion to them, most of them were not that mad, or happy to accept the truth of their issues.

This job gave me a lot of inspiration. Dealing with so many customers a day helps me understand that everyone has different backgrounds and stories. Even though you have a standard procedure to follow, it still works different way for each one of them. Therefore, I believe that you cannot expect to please every passenger, but you can do one small thing to make their day better. It might be nothing to you, but it will mean a lot for them. Now I can say I am a mature and considerate person as well. I try to put myself in someone else's shoes. I hope I can bring this kind of consideration on board to passengers as well. Thank you.

▶▶▶ 中譯

大家早安，我是 Kate，來自馬來西亞。我之前做了兩年的中華航空地勤。我能講流利的馬來話、中文還有英文。除了處理有關航空業務之外，我的工作內容主要是與乘客溝通，因此我是一個很可靠、懂得變通和樂觀的人。在工作的時候常常會遇到一些因為飛行作業沒安排好而比較情緒化的乘客，除了跟他們道歉之外，我會盡我所能想辦法幫他們安排後續的問題。經過我的建議之後，大部份的乘客都能冷靜下來，或者是開心地接受他們所遇到的飛行問題。

這個工作給了我很多啟發，每天處理這麼多乘客的業務讓我瞭解到，每個乘客都有不同的背景和故事，就算有標準程序要照著處理，用在不同乘客身上也會有不同的結果。因此我相信，你沒有辦法期待取悅每個乘客，但是你可以做一小件事情，改變他們的一天。對你來說這可能沒有什麼，不過對乘客來說有可能是事情的轉機。現在我可以說我是一個深思熟慮而且很善解人意的人，我試著站在對方的立場思考。我希望能將這種體貼帶上飛機，服務給每一位乘客。謝謝。

🛫 重點解析

❶ 在介紹自己的名字時，除了可以說 I am +名字之外，許多外國人會用類似電話用語的方式來打招呼。通常我們接起電話時不會說 I am 名字，只會以 this is 某某某、或 this is she 等等。下次在自我介紹的時候，不妨可以以 it is +名字來介紹自己，除了不會顯得很死板外，it's +名字也是很口語跟親切的介紹方式。

❷ despite 雖然／儘管

despite 雖然／儘管…，despite 是介系詞不是連接詞，這邊要特別注意接在後面的必須是名詞，例如 Despite of the typhoon, he came for the conference，如果要連接句子的話，必須加上 despite the fact that...。除此之外也可以用 in spite of 來替代，如：In spite of the typhoon, he came for the conference。兩者都有雖然的意思，不過 in spite of 的語氣較強。另外 despite 當作名詞使用的時候，表示怨恨的意思，要特別小心不要用錯了。

❸ except for... 除了…之外

在使用 except for...除了…之外時，要特別注意其與 except 之間的用法。except 也是除了…之外的意思，不過 except 後面接的通常是同類事物之間的關係，後面能接上的詞性包括名詞、代名詞、副詞、子句等等。如：I exercise everyday except Sunday. 此為後面接名詞，She always eats vegetarian except recently.此為後面接副詞。而 except for 的用法為對於局部做否定，它不用於同類事物間的關係。如：It was a good movie except for the opening. 另外，except for 也可以以 except that +子句替換。如：Everything in the restaurant was good except that the lights were too dark.

❹ 動名詞當主詞

Dealing with so many customers a day helps me understand that everyone has different background and stories. 在這個句子裡，deal 處理，變成動名詞當主詞用，以動名詞當主詞用的句型很常見，但要注意的是，若以動名詞當主詞時，後面的動詞必須是第三人稱單數。而在這裡後面接的動詞 help 就是以第三人稱單數 helps 出現。

自我介紹 5

Track 05

Hello everyone, it's Jack from Taiwan. I am 21 years old, and just graduated from college. I majored in social work, and I have some experience about being a social worker in the home for the aged. I also work part time in a coffee shop. I am outgoing, warm-hearted, and easy-going, which are all related to my previous experiences.

When I was in the home for the aged, I used to deal with their entertainment. My job was to play games with them, teach them to read, and the most important part: talk to them, regardless of the topic. Most of the time, I would just ask them to talk about whatever they wanted to talk about. I am a good listener. For me, to accompany them was the point of being there. Therefore, being considerate is my advantage. On the other hand, reading people's emotions is also my strength.

I like to interact with or take care of people. This is one of the reasons I chose to study social work. I think it is a way to get to know some skills to take care of people. Taking care of people makes me feel warm and of course I hope they will feel the same as me. I hope my enthusiasm and skills for taking care of people will help a lot onboard. I would love to spread this warmth to every passenger I serve.

▶▶▶ 中譯

大家好我是 Jack，來自台灣。我今年 21 歲，剛從大學畢業。我主修社會工作，也有一些在老人之家幫忙的經驗。另外，我也在咖啡店裡打工。我外向、溫暖而且很好相處，而這些個性都跟我過去的活動或打工經驗有相當的關係。

我在老人之家幫忙的時候，負責的是娛樂的部分。我的工作是和他們玩一些簡單的小遊戲、教他們閱讀，最重要的是陪他們講話，不管什麼話題都可以。通常我會讓他們聊他們想講的東西，我是一個很好的傾聽者。對我來說，最重要的是在老人之家陪伴他們。因此，體貼是我一個很大的優點。此外，我也很會察覺人的情緒。

我喜歡和人互動也喜歡照顧人們，這也是我選社會工作系的原因，我認為可以在這個領域中學到一些照顧人時的技巧。照顧人讓我感覺到溫暖，當然我相信對方也會有一樣的感受。希望我對照顧人的熱情和技巧可以在飛機上幫上很多忙，我很願意將這種溫暖散佈給每一位乘客。

✈ 重點解析

❶ related to 有關聯的、親屬關係

在上述中，r e l a t e d t o 是和某事物有關聯的，如：My personalities are related to my job.（我的個性和工作是有關聯的。）而常被搞混的字 relevant to 意思也是有關聯的，不過用法不太一樣。r e l e v a n t t o 指的是關連性不高的關係，His personality is not relevant to his scores in school.（他的個性和他的在校成績不相關。）大家要小心想要表達兩事是高度相關的時候，不要用到 relevant to 了。

❷ deal with... 處理

deal with 為處理某事的意思，其後面也可以接人為受詞，如：His job is to deal with different kinds of customers，deal with 可以表示處理具體亦或抽象的事情，如：I have to deal with my financial problems lately.（我最近必須處理我的財務問題。）與之混淆的片語 cope with 也是處理的意思，不過 cope with 指的是處理較嚴重的事情，而且 cope with 後面的受詞不能接人物。如：Some people find it hard to cope with death.（有些人發現面對死亡很困難。）

❸ tell apart 分辨

Telling apart people's emotion is also my strength. tell apart 是分辨、察覺的意思，在這裡也可以用 be aware of 替代，意思都是能輕易察覺別人的情緒。

❹ strength / advantage 優點

在自我介紹的時候一定會提及自己的優點，如果想要使用優點相關單字可以有以下選擇：advantages 優勢／strength 強項／strong points 長處／forte 專長等，而其分別不同的地方是，advantages 指的比較偏向優勢，在和別人比較之後自己在某方面所佔的優勢；strength 和 srtong points 指的都是自己在某方面的長才；而 forte 則是專指某特定方面的專長。

❺ onboard 在…交通工具上

onboard / aboard / abroad 是常常長得很像會搞混的單字，但他們的意思都不盡相同。onboard 和 aboard 指的是在某個交通工具上，例如火車、船或飛機上，如：I am now onboard the train to the other city.（我現在搭火車去其他城市。）；abroad 指的則是在國外，如：He used to study abroad and now he is back.（他之前在國外念書，現在回來了。）

✈ 自我介紹 6

 Track 06

Good morning everyone, I'm Grace. I am sociable, conscientious and I like to experiment. I like to exercise, including yoga, jogging and swimming. I enjoy eating, and my hobby is to find delicious food all around the city. I majored in English and Journalism when I was in college. After graduation, I was a journalist for three years. Exploring new things and writing stories about different people is my interest and was also my profession.

I learned a lot while being a journalist. This job makes me more open-minded. I have interviewed so many different kinds of people. They all come from different backgrounds. All they want is their voice to be heard. Whenever I face people, I can always find ways to talk to them, being a really good listener. I cannot pretend that I can feel exactly how my interviewers feel, but at least I can put myself in their shoes and give respect to them. This is what I learned, be respectful and understanding in any situation.

Now I want to keep on exploring new things in the world. Therefore, I would like to be part of a cabin crew to meet different people. I am greatly assured that being part of a cabin crew also requires being understanding and respectful in each kind of situation. I hope I can do my best to help onboard. Thank you.

▶▶▶ 中譯

大家早安，我是 Grace。我是一個善於交際、盡責且喜歡冒險的人。我喜歡運動，包括做瑜伽、跑步還有游泳。我也喜歡享受美食，我的興趣之一是在城市到處尋找好吃的食物。我之前在大學的時候主修英文以及新聞學，畢業之後我當了三年的記者。探索新事物還有記錄不同人物的故事是我的興趣，同時也是我的專業。

在擔任記者的期間我學到很多，這個工作讓我變成一個心胸更開闊的人。我訪問過很多不一樣的人，他們都來自不同背景，唯一相同的是他們都想要自己的聲音被聽見。每次我面對人群當聽眾時，我會用一個客觀、尊重還有同理心的態度面對。我雖然不能假裝我可以感覺受訪者的心情，但至少我可以站在他們的立場思考，並且尊重他們的處境。這就是我最大的收穫，在任何狀況下都抱持著尊重和同理心。

現在我想要繼續探索世界上新的事物，因此我想要成為一個空服員。我很確定擔任空服員也需要對於乘客的同理心以及尊重，我希望我可以盡我最大的努力幫助飛機上的乘客，謝謝。

🛩 重點解析

❶ interest / hobby 興趣

自我介紹的時候常需提及自己的興趣，interest 跟 hobby 經常被混淆著使用，兩者同樣是興趣／嗜好的意思，不過在用法上還是有些許差異。interest 指涉的範圍比較廣泛，表示某個人對某項事物有興趣，但是不一定會付諸行動，例如某個人可以對詩歌有興趣，但不會天天都研究或閱讀詩歌；hobby 是比較小範圍的嗜好，hobby 可以被包含在 interest 裡面，表示某個人對某件事物有興趣並且會付諸行動，另如收集郵票就可以是一種 hobby，一個人必須付諸行動去收集郵票才能構成 hobby。大家在使用上還是要注意這個些微的差別。

❷ put myself in someone's shoes 站在別人的立場

put oneself in someone's shoes 是一個很實用的片語，表示站在別人的立場思考，也可以說 stand in someone's shoes、put somebody in someone else's place 等等。在自我介紹的時候是一個很好的片語表達自己的個人特質。

❸ **keep on doing something** 持續做某件事

keep on doing something 也是很常見的用法，它和 keep 的用法類似但有些許不同。如果要表示一個反覆發生的事情時，可以使用 keep 或 keep on，如：It keeps (on) raining.；如果表示一個持續的動作，中間沒有中斷的話則要用 keep，如：She keeps talking about her new boyfriend this afternoon.；如果表示一直在做的事情並且要繼續做下去的話，則要使用 keep on，就如同本文中所提到，如：Now I want to keep on exploring new things in the world.，文中主角已經提及她不斷的在探索新事物，所以繼續探索的話則用 keep on doing something 最為適當。

❹ **assured that...** 深信…

在這裡 assured that 表示相信著…，也可以用 convinced that...、believe that... 代替，代表的都是相信著某事的意思。

自我介紹 7

 Track 07

Good morning everyone, I am Jenny from Hong Kong. I can speak Cantonese, Mandarin, and English well. It is my last year in college. I major in Japanese and I studied in Japan as an exchange student for a year. I love different cultures especially Japanese culture. I can now speak and read Japanese fluently.

During college, I worked for my professor as a research assistant. My job was to assist the professor in research papers, finding resources for papers, reading related papers and report key points to the professor and so on. This job was mainly to assist the research while it's needed. I am a very punctual, responsible, and highly motivated person. I never delayed work; in fact I always handed in papers before the deadline.

On the other hand, I was an interpreter for an exhibition of education. It was an exhibition providing information for students who want to study abroad. There were a lot of universities introducing their courses, environment and the life there. I was responsible for interpreting to those who wanted to know the information but couldn't fully understand English. Therefore, I am also good at being a listener. I can catch others points precisely. After graduation, I really want to keep on exploring and being in touch with different cultures. So I would really appreciated if I could be part of this big cabin crew family. I hope my personality and skills will help on board. Thanks for listening.

▶▶▶ **中譯**

各位早安，我是 Jenny，來自香港，我可以講廣東話、中文和英文。這是我大學的最後一年，我主修日文並且在日本交換了一年。我很喜歡接觸不同的文化，特別是日本文化，現在我可以說跟閱讀流利的日文。

我在大學的時候擔任教授的研究助理。我的工作是協助教授尋找論文、尋找相關資料、閱讀論文並提報告等等，這個工作主要是在教授有需要研究方面的協助時提供幫忙。我是一個很準時、負責且積極主動的人，我從來不會遲交工作，事實上我總是在期限截止之前提早完成。

另一方面，我曾經擔任教育展的口譯人員。這個教育展提供那些想要出國遊學的學生各個大學的資訊，在展覽上不同的大學介紹包括他們的課程、環境還有那邊的生活。我是負責幫忙想要瞭解資訊，英文卻不是那麼流利的同學翻譯給大學的負責人聽，因此，我也是一個很好的傾聽者，我能快速精準地抓到重點。畢業之後，我想要繼續接觸探索不同的文化，所以如果有機會能成會空服員的一份子我會非常感激。我希望我的個人特質還有技能在高空中能帶來很大的助益，謝謝你。

重點解析

❶ during 用法

during 表示在…期間，如：I was studying English during the summer vacation.，要特別注意的是，for 也能表示一段時間，不過 for 指的是持續了多長的一段時間，如：I have been studying English for 2 years.，在此例句中就不能以 during 替代。而在文中 during 也可以用 in 替代，in 也可表示某個時間點的意思。

❷ in fact 事實上

in fact 和 actually 都可以用來表示事實上…，不過在表達語意上是有差別的。in fact 是用來補充前述的句字，通常是一個對前句的肯定和補充，如：Never delayed work, in fact I always hand in papers before deadline.；不過 actually 是用在和前述的句子有相反意見的時候，通常是來修正前述的句子，如：I am not from Korea, actually, I am from Japan.。

❸ responsible for 負責

responsible 通常和 for 連用，表示對…事情負責，後面接名詞或動名詞，如：I am responsible for the finance of this affair.。若是要表達對於…人負責的話，後面接的介系詞則要改成 to，如：I am responsible to my students as a teacher.，除此之外 responsible for 也可解釋為某件事情的原因，如：The typhoon was responsible for the late departure.

❹ **therefore** 因此、所以

therefore 在這邊也可以以 thus, so, hence 替代，都有所以的意思。在自我介紹的時候可以多使用不同的詞替換，才不會讓人覺得一直聽到重複的詞很呆板。

✈ 自我介紹 **8**

 Track 08

Hello everyone, I am Wesley. I am now working as an assistant supervisor of marketing and PR at an international hotel. My duty is to create, coordinate and launch commercial campaigns which might be videos, text or images. I am also the link between the media, partners, and suppliers. By communicating with all kinds of customers, I have learned how to get the main points and meet customer's expectations, while thinking fast and still paying attention to the details.

I am an outgoing, positive, and sociable person. I love to meet people and hear their different stories. I always strive to uncover their needs and help them achieve their goals. Therefore, I chose to attend a workshop which contains a variety of people from different countries in Sweden. We discuss different topics and find out solutions everyday. I enjoyed it a lot, since people everywhere think differently and have a big diversity of opinions. Together, we communicate, negotiate, and compromise with each other. It is interesting to listen to others' thoughts while also giving out my own. Till the end, we share our opinions and figure out the most efficient answer.

Now I am looking for something even more interesting and challenging, to meet people all around the world while working. Thus, I want to become member of a cabin crew. I believe my enthusiasm can bring a lot of fun on board. Of course with my previous experience, I will also get customers' points immediately and meet their expectations. Thank you for your patience. I look forward to hearing from you again.

▶▶▶ 中譯

大家好，我是 Wesley，我現在的工作是一間國際飯店的行銷和公關的執行助理，我的工作內容是發想、協調還有辦理商業活動，像是影片、文字或影像，同時我也是公司和媒體、夥伴和供應商之間的連結。透過跟各式不同的客戶溝通，我學會怎麼樣立刻抓住談話重點，也能達到客戶的期許，而在快速思考的同時也不會忘記小細節。

我是一個外向、正面且善於社交的人，我喜歡認識不同的人並且了解他們的故事。我希望發現他們的需求，然後幫助他們達到他們的目標。因此，我曾經參加一個瑞典工作坊，在那裡有各國不同的人，我們每天都有不同的主題要討論，並且找出共識或者解決的辦法。我很享受當來自各地的人聚集在一起，他們各自有各自的意見並且思考的方式都很不一樣。我們一起溝通、協商還有配合，在你聆聽別人的意見時你也發表自己的意見，這是很有趣的，最後我們有了共識並且找出最有效率的答案。

現在我在追尋更有趣且有挑戰性的事情，那就是在工作時遇見來自世界各國的人。因此，我想要成為一名空服員，我想信我的熱情可以在高空中帶來很多樂趣，當然結合我過去的經驗，我也能夠快速地瞭解乘客需要什麼並且達成他們的期待。謝謝您們的耐心，期待盡快得到您們的回應。

重點解析

❶ a variety of 各式各樣的

a variety of 表示很多不同的、各式各樣的，如：I have a variety of interests.，同時也可以用 various 代替，如：I have various interests.，大家要特別小心的是 various 和 different 的差別，various 強調的是「很多」、「不一樣的」，如：There are various ways to make a tea.（煮茶有各式各樣不同的方式。），而 different 則是強調「不一樣」而不見得是「很多」，如：This tea is different from the others.（這種茶跟其他種茶喝起來很不一樣。）因此，大家在使用的時候記得這些許的差異，如果想要表達各式各樣的則要使用 various 喔！

❷ look for 尋找

look for / search / find 都有尋找的意思，search 一樣是尋找的意思，不過 search 用在較嚴肅、徹底尋找的意思，如：I lost my earrings; I am searching for it.（我弄丟了耳環，我正在找它。）look for 和 find 時常可以互相替代，如：I am looking for a job. 意同於 I am finding a job.，不過在某些語意上是無法通用的如：I found someone to help with my research.（我找到人可以幫忙我的研究。），在這裡無法用 I looked for someone to help with me research.，在這裡 find 指的是尋找過後的結果，如果替換成 look for 的話，語句則會改變成，我之前在找人幫忙我的研究。

❸ look forward to 期待、盼望

look forward to 是期待、盼望的意思，在自我介紹或履歷中是一個很實用的片語，常見的句子為 I look forward to seeing you again.，意思是希望能再次見到對方，表示能夠成功被錄取的意思。不過 look forward to 後面的動詞很常以錯誤的型態被大家使用，如：I look forward to see you again.，大家習慣在 to 後面接上動詞的原形，不過在這邊 to 是介系詞，後面應該要加名詞(n.)，如果是接動詞的話就要轉換成動名詞(Ving)，如：I look forward to seeing (Ving) you again.（我期待能再見到你。），或者是如：I look forward to the graduation ball (n.).（我很期待畢業舞會。）

✈ 自我介紹 9

 Track 09

Good afternoon everyone, I am Anthony from France. I am a positive, adventurous, and considerate person. I had been traveling in Asia for two years. During this time, I'd been to Korea, Japan, China, Singapore, Malaysia and Thailand. I spend two years getting to know very different cultures apart from Europe, but it still wasn't enough. I would love to keep on traveling for no reason just to get closer to the various parts of the world. Hence, I hope I can become a member of cabin crew to fulfill this dream.

I spent three months in Malaysia helping a family to reconstruct their hotel. It was such an interesting job. I didn't even know anyone of them, but I just went and offered to help; therefore, I can have a place to stay and to live as a local also. I love to help people. I like to help them fulfill their dreams. When seeing their faces full of satisfaction, I feel happy as well. During this time living with the locals in Malaysia, I learned a lot about their culture. This is not a thing that tourists will ever learn. I am really thankful for what I have been encountering. I hope I can carry on this kind of open minded attitudes to embrace the whole world. Thanks for your time, I really appreciate it.

▶▶▶ 中譯

大家午安，我是來自法國的 Anthony，我是一個正面、富冒險精神且體貼的人。我曾經在亞洲獨自旅行了兩年，在這段時間我到過韓國、日本、中國、新加坡、馬來西亞還有泰國。我花了兩年了解和歐洲很不相同的文化，但我還是覺得不滿足。我希望可以繼續旅遊，不為了什麼，只為了能更了解這多樣化的世界。因此，我希望可以當一名空服員來實現我的夢想。

在馬來西亞的那三個月，我幫忙一個家庭重建他們的旅館，這是一個超級酷的工作。在還沒去之前，我完全不認識他們，我就是去了、遇到他們然後提供協助。也因為這樣，我在馬來西亞有一個地方可以住，並且像當地人一樣的生活。我喜歡幫助別人，還有完成他們的夢想，看到他們臉上滿足的表情，我自己也能感到很快樂。在和馬來西亞當地人生活的這段時間，我瞭解了很多他們的文化，這是一個觀光客絕對不會體會到的。因此我真的很感謝一路上我所遇到的事情，我希望我可以繼續用這種開闊的心胸擁抱這個世界。謝謝你撥冗聽我介紹，真的很感謝。

重點解析

❶ spend 花

spend / cost / take 都是花費的意思，不過花費的東西不一樣，分別是錢、時間／錢／以及時間。spend 可以是花費「金錢」或者「時間」，但主詞必須是人，如：I spend two years learning Chinese.（我花了兩年學中文。），又或 I spend 100 dollars to buy his present.（我花了100美金買他的禮物。）前後句分別是花費時間以及金錢。cost 只能用來指花費的「金錢」，主詞必須是物品，如：It cost me 100 dollars to buy his present.（買他的禮物花了我100元美金。）take 則適用於花費「時間」，可以用虛主詞或動名詞當主詞，如：It takes me 3 hours to finish this painting. 或 Painting took me three hours to complete.（我花了三小時完成這幅畫。）

❷ fulfill 實現

fulfill one's dream 表示實現某個人的夢想，fulfill 也可以以 realize 替代，realize one's dream 一樣是實現某人夢想的意思。

❸ such 如此的

so 和 such 都是如此的意思，不過在用法上不盡相同。so 後面通常接的是副詞或形容詞，如：The weather today is so nice，而 such 後面則要放名詞，如：Such a nice weather today.，同樣是形容今天天氣很好卻有兩種說法，大家在使用上的時候也要特別小心用法喔。

自我介紹 10

 Track 10

Good morning everyone, I am Zoe from Taiwan. I love to travel. I have been on a cabin crew for Air Asia these two years; therefore, I was living in Malaysia for two years. During my employment, I met different kinds of people. When people work abroad especially by themselves, they will adapt to the life there very quickly. So do I. I adapted to Malaysian life very fast and I really enjoyed it. For me, traveling around while working and living there not only makes this job interesting but also refreshing.

While working on board, I like to chat with passengers. I like to hear their stories and know about different life. The most important thing is that I enjoy the feeling of sharing with someone else. Sharing is caring. I can deeply feel the concept of the word. I love to share. Sharing makes me satisfied and happy. On the other hand, sharing can also be a kind of taking care of people. Therefore, I like to take care of people as well. Combining these two personality traits, taking care of people and traveling around, being a cabin crew member is the ideal job for me. And I believe with my enthusiasm, passengers on board will be well taken care of. Thank you.

▶▶▶ 中譯

大家早安，我是來自台灣的 Zoe。這兩年我在亞航擔任空服員，所以我在馬來西亞生活了兩年，在任職亞航空姐的這段期間，我認識了很多不一樣的人們。當人們在國外工作，尤其是單獨一個人的時候，他們能夠很快地就適應當地的生活，就像我一樣，我很快就適應了馬來西亞的生活，而且還很喜歡。對我來說，不只是到處旅遊很有趣，在一個完全不一樣的環境裡生活更是一件新鮮的事。

我在飛機上工作時，我喜歡和乘客聊天，我喜歡聽他們的故事，了解他們的生活，最重要的是我很喜歡和別人分享的感覺。我很能體會「分享就是一種照顧。」這句話的涵義，我喜歡分享，分享讓我覺得滿足和快樂，另一方面，分享也可以是照顧他人的一種形式，因此我也喜歡照顧別人。結合喜歡照顧他人和到處旅遊這兩種人格特質，空服員對我來說是一個再美好不過的工作。我也相信飛機上的乘客都能因為我的熱情受到很好的照顧。謝謝。

 重點解析

❶ especially 特別是

especially 和 specially 的意思都是特別是⋯，但在用法上有些許差異。especially 通常是指多個狀況、人物裡面你想要特別強調某一個選項，如：Everyone loves the birthday cake, especially the kids.，especially 通常不會出現在句首；specially 則是用來表示為了某個目的而採用的方式，如：I made this cake specially for you. 指我用特別的食譜為你做了這個蛋糕，可能你不吃蛋，所以蛋糕裡我沒加蛋；若是 I made this cake especially for you. 則指我是特地為了你做這個蛋糕。

❷ adapt to 適應

adapt to 是適合、適應、改編的意思，因拼法很像所以常常與 adopt（採取、收養）這個字搞混，不過兩個字意思差很多，千萬不要使用錯了。如：This movie was adapted from a novel.（這部電影改編自小說。）、如：He tries hard to adapt to his new life in college, and he succeed.（他努力適應大學新生活，然後他成功了。）；This couple adopted three children from the care center.（這對夫婦從育樂中心領養了三名小孩。）；He adopted a new way to adapt to his new life.（他採用了新的方式去適應新生活。）

❸ enjoy 樂於、享受

在自我介紹的時候，常常會提到自己熱衷於做什麼事情，enjoy 是很實用的詞彙。不過在使用 enjoy 的時候要特別注意後面動詞的狀態。在 enjoy 後面如果接上動詞的話，則要轉變詞性成動名詞，如：I enjoy watching movies.（我喜歡看電影。）有一點容易被誤會的是，大家可能想說既然動詞要轉成動名詞接在 enjoy 後面，那我直接在動詞前面加上 to 就好了，如：I enjoy to watch movie. 這樣的說法是錯誤的，enjoy 後面只能接動名詞。

2-5　面試廣播詞

✈ 面試廣播詞／機上廣播

　　廣播詞是國內航空公司必考的內容，中文、英文、台語的廣播詞都是常見題型。這個部分是最容易準備及拿分的，大家千萬要把握廣播詞的部分，只要在家裡做好練習，面試時輕鬆大方地唸出來通常都可以獲得不錯的印象。

✈ 面試念廣播詞注意事項

　　在面試時最大的敵人就是緊張，常有許多平時表現很優異的考生因為緊張而在關鍵時刻失敗了。所以最重要的是放鬆、讓心情保持在一個最平穩的狀態，才能將平常的實力展現出來。

▶▶▶ 1. 深吸一口氣

　　念廣播詞前先深吸一口氣，調整自己的呼吸也在這小段的時間裡讓自己冷靜下來。若是呼吸平穩了，句子唸起來會順暢許多，斷句才會有節奏。

▶▶▶ 2.掃描一遍

　　拿到廣播稿之後，先用幾秒鐘大略的把整段看完，這樣一來比較瞭解內容在說什麼，在唸的時候除了對內容沒那麼陌生之外，通常大腦會幫剛剛快速掃瞄的句子記憶下來，當你在唸這句的時候心裡就會有底下一句大概是什麼，唸的時候比較不會因為對稿生疏而打結。

▶▶▶ 3.不必刻意想達到完美的捲舌

　　很多人對於廣播詞都有刻板印象，就是要唸得非常字正腔圓，所以常常追求把每個捲舌音都唸得很標準，不過太刻意反而會造成反效果，越是想要把這個字念很標準，就越會影響到整句的順暢度。把字唸正確、態度自信、適當的地方斷句（換氣）就是最好的表達方式。

▶▶▶ 4.調整音量

　　相信有些考生平常講話音量沒那麼大聲，不過在面試的時候千萬要調整音量了，畢竟面試官坐在前面一排並不是貼在你旁邊聽你朗誦廣播詞，所以要想辦法讓整間考場都聽得到你的音量。但也不要因為想要唸得大聲而就用吼的，這樣是沒有辦法達到效果的，而且很容易就沒有氣。音量較小的朋友除了練習廣播詞的內容外，也要練習控制自己的音量，久而久之讓自己習慣念廣播詞就是需要這個音量，在面試時才不會因為環境不同而有所變化。

▶▶▶ 5.調整音調

　　在念廣播詞時音調也是很重要的因素，大家可以找朋友練習聽聽看自己念廣播詞的音量是否能讓對方清楚了解，太高、太低的音量都會影響聽者理解的能力。

▶▶▶ 6.速度

人們在講話時，因為是很口語的東西所以速度會比唸稿子快很多，大家在念廣播詞的時候千萬不要像平時在講話一樣，批哩啪拉一下就把它唸完。放慢速度，從容不迫地把它念完才能讓考官聽得清楚又不會有壓迫感唷。

機上做廣播時的注意事項

除了上述面試時念廣播詞要注意的特點之外，在機上做廣播更要額外細心。由於飛機上走來走去的人很多，又或是乘客、廚房或是引擎的聲音很大聲，往往在收音的時候會有很多背景雜音，因此大家在做機上廣播的時候盡量遠離那些雜音的來源，除了讓乘客能清楚聽到廣播之外，也不讓機上廣播聽起來不專業。另外，由於機上廣播是由麥克風通過廣播系統發送出去的，所以就像拿麥克風在講話一樣，避免把嘴巴靠得太近以免噗麥。

機艙廣播

機艙廣播的目的是為了清楚地傳達各種有關飛機上的服務或是安全措施給乘客，是一個飛行中很重要的環節，萬一發生緊急事故也必須用廣播向乘客說明狀況，也因此空服人員上飛機後第一個檢查的就是廣播設備。

▶▶▶ 2-5-1 Captain's PA　　　　　　　⊙ Track 11

Ladies and gentlemen, this is ＿＿＿＿ (captain's name) your captain speaking. First of all, I would like to welcome everyone on board ＿＿＿＿ (flight number) flight to ＿＿＿＿ (destination).

We will first climb up to ＿＿＿＿ ft, then cruise at ＿＿＿＿ ft (flight altitude). The weather is fine on the way, just a few bumps when we pass over India. I would like you to keep seatbelt on at all times for safety. Now just sit back, relax and enjoy the flight.

▶▶▶ 機長廣播

各位乘客，這是機長 ＿＿＿＿（機長名字）廣播，首先歡迎大家搭乘這班 ＿＿＿＿（班機號碼）班機前往 ＿＿＿＿（目的地）。

我們會先爬升到 ＿＿＿＿（飛行高度）英尺然後航行於 ＿＿＿＿（飛行高度）英尺。一路上天氣都很好，只是在經過印度上方時會有一些不穩定氣流。基於安全考量，請您全程都將安全帶繫上。現在請您放輕鬆，盡情享受我們的航班。

▶▶▶ 小提示

一般來說機長對乘客的廣播次數並不多，只有在要起飛時即降落前會做廣播。在乘客登機後首先會由機長廣播歡迎全體乘客，並且簡單報告今天的飛行資訊，像是爬行高度、氣候等，主要是報告飛行資訊，並且期待乘客有一個美好的旅程。

▶▶▶ 2-5-2 Welcome PA

🔘 Track 12

Good morning (afternoon / evening) ladies and gentlemen, I'm _____ (cabin crew's name), I would like to welcome you on board _____ (flight number) flight to _____ (destination). The flying time is_____ hrs _____ mins.

We are now ready for take-off. Please switch off your laptop and put it in the overhead compartment Other electronic devices such as mobile phones, e-readers and tablets must be in airplane mode, or switched off.

We remind you that this is a non-smoking flight. Smoking is prohibited on board the entire aircraft, including the lavatories.

▶▶▶ 歡迎廣播

各位貴賓早安（午安／晚安），我是 ＿＿＿＿（空服員姓名），非常歡迎您搭乘 ＿＿＿＿（班機號碼）班機前往 ＿＿＿＿（目的地），飛行時間為 ＿＿＿＿ 小時 ＿＿＿＿ 分鐘。

我們正準備起飛，請您將手提電腦放在座位上方的行李艙內，其他電子用品像是手機、平板電腦、電子書則要保持在飛航模式或關機狀態。

本班機是禁菸航班，在客艙包含廁所內吸菸是違法的行為。

▶▶▶ 小提示

在每個航班登機差不多完成的時候，會聽到一個歡迎的廣播。隨著當地時間而有不同的問候語，並且會提及本班機的航空及班號，以及前往的目的地。歡迎廣播每家航空大同小異，除了歡迎詞外接下來就是準備要起飛請乘客們遵守安全規定，並且會接著播放安全影片。

1 招考資訊

2 100%應試準備教戰

3 空服員飛行英語日記

4 附錄

▶▶▶ 2-5-3 Dim Light PA
Track 13

Ladies and gentlemen, we are going to dim the lights for night time take-off (landing). If you wish to read, the light is by your seat. Thank you.

▶▶▶ 熄燈廣播（夜間起飛／降落）

各位貴賓，根據夜間起飛（降落）需求，我們將調整客艙內燈光，如果您想要繼續閱讀，可以使用座位上方的閱讀燈。謝謝。

▶▶▶ 小提示

客艙內如果太亮的話會影響飛行員起飛和降落，因此在夜間起飛的話會聽到這個廣播，意思就是會將客艙內的燈光調暗，但是乘客還是可以繼續使用座位上方的閱讀燈。

▶▶▶ 2-5-4 Mobile Using PA

Track 14

Ladies and gentlemen, you may now use your mobile phone, SMS services, and laptop. Please set your mobile phone to vibrate or silent as a courtesy to others.

▶▶▶ 手機使用廣播

各位乘客，您現在可以使用手機、SMS 服務以及手提電腦了。請將您的電子用品調整為靜音或振動模式，以維護他人權益。

▶▶▶ 小提示

這個 PA 不一定每個航班都會聽到，有些航班在起飛過後可以正常使用手機才會有此廣播。另外，也有可能在穿越不同區域的領空時暫停手機服務會多做說明。

▶▶▶ 2-5-5 Turbulence PA Track 15

Ladies and gentlemen, we are now passing through an area of turbulence. Please return to your seat, fasten your seatbelts and refrain from using the lavatories at this time.

▶▶▶ 亂流廣播

各位乘客，我們正通過一段不穩定的氣流，請您返回座位，繫上安全帶並不要在此時使用廁所，謝謝合作。

▶▶▶ 小提示

在安全帶警示燈亮起之後，一定要做這個廣播，表示我們有可能（已經）穿越一股亂流，以確保乘客們的安全。

▶▶▶ 2-5-6 Landing PA 　　　　　🔘 Track 16

Ladies and gentlemen, we are starting our final descent. Please put your seat backs and tray tables in the fully upright and locked position, and open the window shades.

Make sure your seat belt is securely fastened and all personal belongings are stowed underneath the seat in front of you or in the overhead bins. Please turn all of your electronic devices to airplane mode or turn them off. Thank you.

▶▶▶ 降落廣播

各位乘客，我們正要降落。請您將座椅調直、收起桌板、打開遮光板。

請確認繫好安全帶，個人物品須放置在座椅上方的行李櫃或是前方座位下面。並請您將所有電子用品調整成飛航或關機狀態，謝謝。

▶▶▶ 小提示

進行最後降落前的 PA，會根據不同機場名字而做更改。

▶▶▶ 2-5-7 After Landing PA

Track 17

Ladies and gentlemen, welcome to _____ Airport. The local time is _____ and the temperature is _____ degrees Celsius.

For your safety, please stay in your seat with your seatbelt fastened until the seat belt sign has been switched off. You can now use your mobile phone.

Please check your seat pocket and overhead bin to make sure you have all your belongings with you. Please open overhead bins with caution as heavy articles may fall out.

If you need any help transferring to another flight, please contact the airport ground staff meeting this flight.

If you need further help, please remain seated until other passengers have deplaned. One of our cabin crew will be happy to assist you you. Thank you.

▶▶▶ 落地廣播

各位乘客，歡迎來到 ＿＿＿（機場名稱）機場。當地時間為 ＿＿＿ 溫度為 ＿＿＿ 度。

為了您的安全，請留在座位上並繫好安全帶，直到安全帶指示燈熄滅為止。您現在可以使用手機了。

離開前請確認椅背口袋和座位上方行李艙，確保帶走所有行李。打開行李艙時請多加留意物品掉落。

如果您需要轉機，請尋求機場人員協助。

若是需要另外的幫助，請留在座位上，待乘客下機後會有空服人員幫忙您，謝謝。

▶▶▶ 小提示

每個航班降落的機場和時間不一樣，空服員常常飛不同時區的國家，所以可能會被時差影響導致時間地點混亂，在這裡要特別小心不要念錯機場名稱以及當地時間。

▶▶▶ 2-5-8 Delay PA

Track 18

Ladies and gentlemen, due to weather / technical / traffic control reasons, we will be departing after _____ (delayed time) mins. We apologize for any inconvenience.

▶▶▶ 延遲廣播

各位乘客，因為氣候／技術／航空管制原因，我們將延遲 _____ 分鐘後出發。造成您的不方便，我們深感抱歉。

▶▶▶ 小提示

班機延誤是很常有的事情，如果延誤時間較長，通常會有廣播說明狀況，像是延誤原因、延誤多久以及致歉等等。

▶▶▶ 2-5-9 Middle East Flights Arrival PA　🔘 Track 19

Ladies and gentlemen, following is an important health announcement from the Taiwan CDC:

In response to the ongoing outbreak and the recent occurrence of Middle East Respiratory Syndrome Coronavirus (MERS-CoV) cases, if you have experienced symptoms such as fever, cough, or diarrhea, please notify the Taiwan CDC quarantine officer at the airport upon your arrival.

If you develop the aforementioned symptoms within 21 days after returning home, please call the toll-free hotline 1922 to seek medical attention and inform the doctor of your recent exposure and travel history. Thank you.

▶▶▶ 中東地區入境航機宣導廣播

各位乘客，以下是來自台灣疾病管制署的提醒：

因應國際間伊波拉及中東呼吸症候群冠狀病毒感染症疫情，如果您有發燒、咳嗽或腹瀉症狀，下機後請主動向疾病管制署機場檢疫人員申報。

返國 21 天內如有身體不適，請撥打免費防疫專線 1922，並立即就醫告知接觸史及旅遊史，謝謝您的合作。

▶▶▶ 小提示

因應國際間的傳染疾病，不同國家都會有不同的聲明稿，並且請入境的航班代為廣播給乘客知道，而這段廣播通常會再出現飛機降落後。近來台灣也因為伊波拉以及 MERS 的緣故而有此廣播。

▶▶▶ 2-5-10 Quarantine / Landing Cards- Australia PA　🔊 Track 20

This is an important message from the Australian Government. Australia has strict biosecurity laws that affect you. Your crew will issue you with two documents, which you must complete. These documents will also be available in the terminal on your arrival.

The first document will be a Travel History Card. This card will ask you if you have travelled to Africa in the past 21 days. The card will also contain important health information on Ebola. It is extremely important that you answer this honestly to protect you, your family, and other members of the community.

If you have travelled to Africa in the past 21 days, you must answer "yes". On the basis of the information provided, you may be identified as being required to attend a quarantine inspection after disembarkation, at a place specified by a quarantine officer. On arrival, provide this card to an official, who will give you directions. A false statement to a Commonwealth public official may result in a penalty.

The second document that you will receive is an Incoming Passenger Card that asks questions about what you are bringing to Australia and the places you have visited.

You must mark "yes" on your Incoming Passenger Card if you have certain food, plant or animal products, or equipment or shoes used in rivers or lakes or with soil attached. Food supplied on board must be left on board.

You must answer this card truthfully, this card is a legal document and a false statement may result in a penalty. It will be checked by an official on your arrival.

After any international travel, there may be a small chance that you have been exposed to a communicable disease. If you are feeling unwell, particularly with fever, chills, or sweats, it is important for your own health and for the protection of others, that you bring this to the attention of a member of the crew. Thanks for your cooperation.

▶▶▶ 入境卡廣播—入境澳洲

以下是澳洲政府的重要訊息。澳洲對於生物安全很嚴格，空服員接下來會發兩份文件。請您務必填完。這些文件也可在航廈拿取。

第一份文件是旅遊史，會問你在過去21天是否到過非洲，以及包含伊波拉的重要健康資訊。請依照詳情填寫，這將會保護你的家人和朋友。

如果你在過去 21 天內有到過非洲，務必填寫「是」。基於你填答的資料，在下飛機後你有可能會被要求至檢疫處檢疫審查。請將文件交由指

示您方向的官員。填寫錯誤的資訊有可能會被罰鍰。

第二份文件是乘客入境卡，填寫關於你帶進澳洲的物品，還有你到過的地方

如果妳有攜帶食物、植物或者是動物產品，又或是在河川湖泊使用過的器具跟鞋子，您必須填答「是」。飛機上提供的食物務必留在飛機上。

你必須據實填寫，以免受罰。抵達後，將有官員檢查您的入境卡。

國際旅行有可能使您接觸到傳染病源，如果你有感到不舒服，像是發燒、發冷、盜汗等，請將此卡交給其中一名空服員，以確保自己及他人健康安全。謝謝合作。

▶▶▶ 小提示

澳洲是一個入境控管很嚴格的國家，包括食物及疾病的入境。任何食物不管是生食、熟食、乾糧等，若有攜帶一定要申報澳洲管制局，如果沒有據實填寫將會受罰。

疾病的管制也是一樣，到過任何地方尤其是非洲都要據實填寫，包含身體不舒服的症狀也要通知澳洲管制局。

▶▶▶ 2-5-11 Non-smoking PA
Track 21

Ladies and gentlemen, this is a non-smoking flight. Smoking is prohibited by law. Tampering with the lavatory smoke detectors is also prohibited by law.

▶▶▶ 禁菸廣播

各位乘客，這是禁菸航班。抽煙是違法的行為，破壞煙霧偵測器同樣是違法的行為，請您配合。

▶▶▶ 小提示

在乘客登機的時候，除了歡迎廣播之外也會說明航班為禁菸航班。不過在航行的過程中，仍會有乘客在廁所偷吸菸，嚴重者還破壞煙霧偵測器。因此，當空服員發現這類狀況發生時，會再度廣播提醒乘客在航班上吸菸是違法的行為。

▶▶▶ 2-5-12 Lost and found PA

Ladies and gentlemen, we have found _____ (found item) in _____ (found location), if it belongs to you, please identify yourself to one of our cabin crew.

▶▶▶ 失物招領廣播

各位乘客，我們在 _____（拾獲地點）找到 _____（拾獲物品），如果是您的物品，請通知我們的空服人員，謝謝。

▶▶▶ 小提示

常會有許多乘客在飛機上掉東西，當然好心的乘客會把它轉交給空服員處理，空格中依遺失的物品做更改，如果是特別貴重的物品，空服員不會把物品名稱講出來，只會以 valuable items 來替代，以免造成每個人都來認領。另外，在航行中有些乘客也許在睡覺會錯過廣播，因此建議在降落前進行最後安全檢查時（大家都醒來時），再進行失物招領。

▶▶▶ 2-5-13 Duty free PA

 Track 23

Ladies and gentlemen, we are now passing through the cabin with a selection of duty free items. Please see the duty free magazine in your seat pocket, and notify our cabin crew if you would like to make a purchase.

▶▶▶ 免稅商品廣播

各位乘客,我們機上有提供免稅商品,在您座椅前方有免稅商品雜誌,請參考雜誌選購並通知我們的空服人員。

▶▶▶ 小提示

在空服員出完餐之後,會進行免稅品的販賣,不過這時候多數的乘客在做自己的事像看電影、睡覺等,因此在空服員進客艙內販售免稅品的時候,會有廣播提醒大家,並告訴大家哪裡可以得知空中免稅品的資訊。

▶▶▶ 2-5-14 Doctor on Board PA　　　🎵 Track 24

Ladies and gentlemen, attention please, if anyone of you is a doctor or medical professional, please notify any one of our cabin crew. Thank you.

▶▶▶ 尋求機上醫生廣播

各位乘客請注意，若您是醫生或醫療人員，請向任何一位我們的空服員表明身份，謝謝。

▶▶▶ 小提示

雖然空服人員都有做過醫療訓練，不過在重大的醫療事件的時候，或許有身份證明的醫生在一旁做指導會更有效率。因此，有時醫療事件除了空服人員進行處理之外，還會向乘客進行廣播尋求醫生的協助。

▶▶▶ 2-5-15 On Ground Transit　⦿ Track 25

Ladies and gentlemen, please return to your seats and identify your luggage to our cabin crew as a part of the transit security. Luggage that is not identified will be off-loaded. Thanks for your cooperation.

▶▶▶ 地面轉機行李指認廣播

各位乘客，基於轉機安全作業，請向我們的空服人員指認您的行李，沒有被指認的行李將會被卸載，謝謝您的合作。

▶▶▶ 小提示

常有很多航班不是直達目的地，有時候中途會在另一個機場停留讓部分乘客可以下機，而另一部分的乘客則是轉機再繼續飛往目的地。某些轉機作業會讓乘客下機再登機，有些則是讓乘客留在機上等待，而在機上等待的旅客則需要指認行李讓空服員知道，以免發生下機乘客忘記帶行李的狀況。

▶▶▶ 2-5-16 Divert PA

🔘 Track 26

Ladies and gentlemen, due to _____ (divert reason) reason, we have to divert into _____ (airport name) airport in _____ minutes. We apologize for any inconvenience. Thank you.

▶▶▶ 轉降其他機場廣播

各位乘客，由於 _____（轉降原因），在 _____ 分鐘後我們將轉降在 _____（機場名稱）機場。 造成您的不方便敬請見諒，謝謝。

▶▶▶ 小提示

飛行會遇到的狀況很多，有時難免遇到無法抗拒的因素導致飛機需要轉降其他機場，像是飛機上有緊急的醫療狀況、飛機上發現不明物體、氣候因素等等，因此，機長一旦決定要轉降其他機場，就會廣播通知乘客轉降資訊。

空服員飛行英語日記

3-1　艙內服務訓練-1：發送熱毛巾

Track 27

T ▶ Trainee 訓練生　P ▶ Pax 乘客　R ▶ Trainer 訓練員

(crew giving out hot towels)　　　　（空服員發送熱毛巾）

T ▶ Hello, sir. Good morning. Would you like a hot towel?

訓練生 ▶ 哈囉，早安。需要熱毛巾嗎？

P ▶ What is it for?

乘客 ▶ 這是做什麼用的？

T ▶ To clean yourself.

訓練生 ▶ 讓您可以清潔自己。

R ▶ Wait, wait, wait. You don't say TO CLEAN YOURSELF while giving out the towels. You can say the towel is to refresh.

訓練員 ▶ 等一下，你不可以跟乘客說是清潔自己用，你可以說這是讓你消除疲勞、提振精神用。

T ▶ Oh, yes, it is for refreshing.

訓練生 ▶ 喔，好。可以讓您恢復精神用。

✈ 單字解析

❶ refresh　*v.*　消除疲勞、提起精神、使清新

The cool water refreshed me after a long walk.

走了一段很長的路之後，一杯冰涼的水讓我恢復精神。

✈ 常用短句

❶ What for? 什麼用途？／為什麼？

當我們在詢問某個東西的用途時可以使用 what for，如：What is this form for?（這個表格是用來幹嘛的？）。另外一種用法是可以代替 why 表示為什麼。如：I am going to London next month. / What for?（我下個月要去倫敦。／為什麼？）。

❷ Would you like to v. / n. ? 你想要…嗎？

當我們在詢問別人意見或提供選擇的時候，常常會用到 would you like to v. / n.（你想要…嗎？）。比如在餐廳會聽到服務生說 Would you like to have some water?（請問您需要水嗎？），而我們在請求幫忙的時候也一樣會用 would like to 來回應。如：I would like a ticket to London please.，記住在回應的時候盡量避免使用 I want something，因為這聽起來比較不客氣。千萬不要當奧客，除了請、謝謝、不好意思之外，在點餐的時候也別忘了用 I would like to have something 而非 I want something 喔！

1 招考資訊

2 100%應試準備教戰

3 空服員飛行英語日記

4 附錄

3-2 艙內服務訓練-2：發送入境卡

Track 28

T ▸ **Trainee** 訓練生　 P ▸ **Pax** 乘客

(Cabin crew is giving out landing cards)

（空服員發送入境卡）

T ▸ Landing cards for Singapore?

訓練生 ▸ 新加坡入境卡？

P ▸ Yes, sorry I don't know if I need one.

乘客 ▸ 不好意思，我不知道我需不需要？

T ▸ Are you going to Singapore or Melbourne?

訓練生 ▸ 您要到新加坡還是墨爾本？

P ▸ I'm transferring in Singapore to Melbourne.

乘客 ▸ 我要在新加坡轉機到墨爾本。

T ▶ Then you don't need one. Only passengers whose final destination is Singapore and don't holding Singaporean passport need one.

訓練生 ▶ 那您不需要新加坡入境卡，只有終點站是新加坡，且不是新加坡市民的旅客才需要入境卡。

P ▶ Do I need to get off the aircraft in Singapore?

乘客 ▶ 那我等下在新加坡需要下飛機嗎？

T ▶ Yes, passengers going to Melbourne are required to leave this aircraft with all your personal belongings and board this craft again. There will be ground staff at the end of the airbridge meeting this flight for the connecting flights.

訓練生 ▶ 要喔，往墨爾本的乘客到新加坡後，需要帶著自己所有的個人物品下飛機並且重新再登機一次。地勤人員會在空橋底端指引需要轉機的乘客。

P ▶ Got it, cheers.

乘客 ▶ 了解了，謝謝！

1 招考資訊

2 100％應試準備教戰

3 空服員飛行英語日記

4 附錄

單字解析

❶ landing cards 入境卡

Foreigners require landing cards while entering another country.

外國人在入境別的國家時需要入境卡。

➤ 入境卡也可說 arrival card、entry card、customs form。

❷ transfer *v.* **轉機**

I will transfer in Hong Kong and then to Bangkok.

我會先在香港轉機，然後到曼谷。

➤ connecting flight 轉機的班機

❸ get off 離開、下⋯（交通工具）

I got off the plane around 4 p.m., now I am on the way to city.

我大概四點的時候下飛機，現在在去市區的路上。

➤ 下飛機也可以用 leave / disembark the aircraft

❹ require *v.* **需要**

All passengers boarding the aircraft are required to show their boarding pass and passport.

所有登機的乘客都必須出示他們的登機證和護照。

❺ hold *v.* 持有

I am holding an Australian passport but my origin is Taiwan.

我持著澳洲護照，但我來自台灣。

➢ 持有某國護照用 hold 這個動詞

✈ 常用短句

❶ How are you? 你好嗎？

外國人見面時最常用也一定會說的招呼語，就像是臺灣人見面時會說的最近過得怎麼樣？最近如何呀？除了 how are you 之外，也常常會聽到外國人說 How are you doing、How is it going、What's up、What have you been up to... 等等都是見面時的問候語。在登機時除了問候早安晚安之外，和乘客說一句 how are you 會顯得更親切，也能簡單開啟你們的對話！

3-3 艙內服務訓練-3：機上送餐

Track 29

T▶ **Trainee 訓練生** P▶ **Pax 乘客**

(during lunch service) （午餐服務）

T▶ Hello, would you like to have lunch?

訓練生▶哈囉，您要吃午餐嗎？

P▶ Yes please.

乘客▶好，謝謝。

T▶ Sir, sorry can I offer you chicken? I ran out of beef today.

訓練生▶先生不好意思，我可以提供您雞肉嗎？牛肉已經發送完了。

P▶ I don't like chicken.

乘客▶我不喜歡雞肉。

T ▶ Sorry about that. I can't promise you anything yet, but if you'd like to wait, I can check it again for you right after the service.

訓練生 ▶ 不好意思，我無法跟您保證一定會有，不過如果您願意等的話，結束午餐服務後我可以幫您確認有沒有多餘的牛肉。

P ▶ It's fine, I will wait.

乘客 ▶ 沒關係，我可以等。

(after 20 mins)

（20 分鐘後）

T ▶ Sir, you are lucky. I checked every oven. It happened to be the last beef.

訓練生 ▶ 先生，很幸運的，我找了所有烤箱，剛好多一個牛肉。

P ▶ Thank you so much. Really appreciate it.

乘客 ▶ 謝謝你。真的很感激。

✈ 單字解析

❶ check   *v.*   確認

I will check the order for you.

我會為您確認一下訂單。

❷ oven   *v.*   爐，灶，烤箱

My Mother took the meatpie out of the oven.

我媽媽將肉派從烤箱中拿出來。

❸ appreciate   *v.*   感激，感謝

She deeply appreciates her professor's kindness and help.

她深深地感激她教授的好意與幫助。

✈ **常用短句**

❶ **happen to be 碰巧、剛好**

表達碰巧發生、預料之外的狀況可以使用 happen to be，例如：
My sister's friend happens to be my flatmate.（我姊姊的朋友剛好是我的室友。）在飛機上若是發生了無法完成乘客要求的狀況，例如換位子、餐點沒有了、乘客想要的東西剛好沒有提供，可以使用 happen to be 做委婉的拒絕。例如，想要雞肉餐但沒有了可以說 Sorry, it happens to be that we finished all the chicken today.（不好意思，雞肉餐剛好沒有了。）又或是，Sorry, it happens to be that it's a full flight today, so there's no more window seat.（不好意思，我們今天剛好滿班，沒有多餘靠窗的位子可以換。）

❷ **run out / run out of 用完、沒有剩下了**

表示某個東西用完了、沒有剩下了，最常見、最實用的用法是表示某項電子用品沒電了，例如：My phone is running out of battery.（我的手機快沒電了。）

❸ **offer someone something / offer to do something 提供**

offer 表示提供的意思，用在願意主動提供幫忙的時候。例如看到別人需要幫忙時可以說，Can I offer you something?（我可以幫些什麼忙嗎？）。

1 招考資訊

2 100%應試準備教戰

3 空服員飛行英語日記

4 附錄

3-4 起飛前巡視機艙

Track 30

C ▶ Cabin Crew 空服員　　**P** ▶ Passenger 乘客

(cabin crew securing the cabin)　　（空服人員巡視機艙）

C ▶ Ladies and gentlemen, we are about to takeoff now. Please return to your seat and make sure all your personal items are under the seat in front of you or in the overhead compartment. Please put the seat back upright, the armrest down and securely fasten your seat belt. Fold away the tray table and open the window blind. Personal electronic devices and mobile phones should be in airplane mode or switched off.

空服員 ▶ 各位先生小姐，我們正準備起飛，請回到您的座位上，確保您所有個人物品放置在前方座位底下或上方的行李櫃裡。請把椅背扶直、座椅扶手放下、並扣好安全帶。餐桌闔上並打開遮光板。所有個人電子用品和手機必須調整到飛航模式或是關機狀態。

Please read the safety card in your seat pocket to ensure you are aware of your nearest exit and the aircraft's safety features.

請詳閱椅背口袋內的安全指示卡確保您熟知飛機的安全設備及最近的緊急出口。

P ▸ Hello, can I use the lavatory now?

乘客 ▸ 你好，我可以去廁所嗎？

C ▸ I'm sorry sir. We are about to take off now. You have to return to your seat and fasten your seatbelt.

空服員 ▸ 對不起我們要起飛了，請您回到座位上並扣好安全帶。

P ▸ Please I am really in a hurry.

乘客 ▸ 拜託，我真的很急。

C ▸ Unfortunately, this is a safety issue sir. I can't let you go to the toilet now. Please go back to your seat until we are at cruising altitude and the seatbelt sign is turned off.

空服員 ▸ 這是安全問題，先生。現在不能使用廁所，請您回到座位上直到飛機到達一定高度且安全帶指示燈熄滅為止。

✈ 單字解析

❶ take off 起飛

The plane took off after all the passengers were onboard.

飛機在所有乘客登機後就起飛了。

➤ landing 降落

❷ return *v.* 返回

Amy returned her tray back to the galley after she had finished the meal.

Amy 用完餐後把餐盤拿到廚房。

❸ cabin *n.* 機艙

The purser is in the cabin talking to the frequent flyers.

座艙長正在機艙內跟飛行常客談話。

➤ purser 座艙長

➤ flight deck 駕駛艙

❹ compartment *n.* 隔層、隔間

Please put your laptop in the overhead compartment.

請把你的筆電放在上方行李櫃裡。

➤ overhead compartment 行李櫃

❺ feature *n.* 特徵、特色

The most famous feature of this aircraft type is its doubled deck.

這架飛機最大的特點就是它是雙層飛機。

➢ safety features 安全設施

❻ device *n.* 設備

All electronic devices should be switched off during taxi, takeoff and landing.

所有電子產品在滑行、起飛及降落的時候都必須關機。

✈ 常用短句

❶ about to 即將

在飛機上常會聽到的片語 about to（即將），飛機準備起飛及降落之前會聽到空服員的廣播，提醒乘客並請他們做好安全準備。例如：Ladies and gentlemen, we are about to land in Taipei international airport, please complete your call.（各位先生女士，我們即將降落在台北國際機場，請結束您的通話。）about to 也是非常生活化的片語，常用來說明自己正要做什麼，比起 soon 更有「正要開始」做某個動作的意涵。如：I am about to sleep, I finished my homework few hours ago.（功課我幾小時前就完成了，我現在正要睡覺了。）

❷ be aware of 注意、警覺

Please read the safety card in your seat pocket, ensuring that you are aware of the safety features of this aircraft.（請閱讀椅背口袋內的安全指示卡，並確保您熟悉這架飛機的安全設施）。當空服員最重要的就是對飛機上的任何事物保有警覺心（be aware of everything），不管發現什麼不尋常都要有警覺，不能把它視為理所當然。因此，乘客也被要求要了解飛機上的安全設備（be aware of the safety features），以防萬一在緊急避難的時候，可以配合空服員的指示，更快速的做緊急逃生。

❸ in a hurry 急切

表示趕時間或非常急迫需要做某件事情。如：I was in a hurry to school, so I didn't have time to pack my lunch box.（今天上學的時候太趕了，沒有時間帶午餐的便當）。

❹ have to 必須

have to 用來表示客觀性的義務，你沒有其他選擇而必須完成這項任務。如：You have to show your boarding pass when entering the aircraft. It's mandatory.（在登機時，你必須出示你的登機證。這是強制的。）

1 招考資訊

2 100%應試準備教戰

3 空服員飛行英語日記

4 附錄

3-5 登機中-1：乘客換位子

Track 31

C ▸ Cabin Crew 空服員　P ▸ Passenger 乘客

C ▸ Good morning, how's it going?

空服員 ▸ 早安，您好嗎？

P ▸ Very good, you?

乘客 ▸ 非常好，你呢？

C ▸ I'm good, thank you.

空服員 ▸ 我很好，謝謝。

P ▸ Do you know if there are any empty seats by any chance or if I can swap seats with anyone?

乘客 ▸ 你知道今天有沒有空的位子，還是我可以跟其他人換位子？

C ▸ We haven't closed the final door for departure, so we still don't know yet. Would you like to swap seats?

空服員 ▸ 我們還沒關最後一個機艙門所以還不確定，您想要換位子嗎？

P ▸ Oh yes, I'm in a window seat now. But my legs were injured last week. I was wondering if I could

乘客 ▸ 對啊，我的是靠窗的位子，可是我的腳上禮拜扭到了，我在想是不是

swap to a bulkhead seat so I can stretch my legs a bit.

可以換到艙壁前面的位子，這樣就有多一點空間可以伸展。

C ▸ Are you alright? Do you need any assistance?

空服員 ▸ 您還好嗎？有需要任何協助嗎？

P ▸ I'm good, thank you. It's just that it would be better for me to have more space for a 10 hours flight.

乘客 ▸ 我很好不用擔心，只是我想說這是 10 小時的航班，如果有多一點空間對我的腳會比較好。

C ▸ I get it. So, sir, if someone is willing to swap with you, you can just swap seats straight away. When the final door is closed and no one is sitting at the bulkhead seat, you can just move there.

空服員 ▸ 我知道了，先生，如果有人願意跟您換位子，您們可以自行交換位子沒有問題。然後等最後一個機艙門關閉之後，如果沒有人坐在艙壁前的位子的話，您可以坐過去。

P ▸ Thank you so much!

乘客 ▸ 謝謝你！

單字解析

❶ swap *v.* 交換

I swapped my duties with others so I can have 3 days off to celebrate Christmas.

我和別人調班了，這樣我就有三天可以慶祝聖誕節。

➢ swap seats 換位子

在飛機上很實用的單字。下次在飛機上想要換位子可以用這個單字喔！

❷ injury *n.* 受傷

He had a very serious head injury after that car accident.

在那場車禍之後他的頭部受到很嚴重的創傷。

❸ bulkhead *n.* 艙壁

I always ask for the bulkhead seat when I'm booking the tickets.

每次買機票的時候，我總會要求要艙壁前面的位子。

➢ bulkhead seat 艙壁前面的位子

➢ window seat 靠窗的位子

➢ aisle seat 靠走道的位子

❹ stretch   *v.*   伸展

She does some stretching exercise everyday before bed.

她每天睡覺前都會做一些伸展運動。

❺ departure   *n.*   出發

We were late for the departure, so we took another flight to London.

我們趕不上飛機出發的時間，所以搭了另一班前往倫敦的飛機。

➢ arrival 抵達

 常用短句

❶ by any chance 碰巧、剛好

在尋求幫忙時，我們會在句中加上 by any chance 讓詢問的口氣聽起來比較客氣。就像是中文裡在尋求別人幫忙，是在人家不介意、不麻煩的狀態下再幫忙的意思一樣。例如，如果你剛好順路的話可不可以幫我投個信件？加上 by any chance 的話比較不會讓人覺得有壓力是剛好有機會才幫忙你的。如：Do you have an extra pen by any chance?（你會不會剛好有多一支筆可以借我？）

❷ wonder if 想知道

當想知道某件事情的時候可以用 wonder if...，同時也是在對別人提出要求時的禮貌性問法。如：I was wondering if you could come to the movie tonight?（我在想你晚上能不能來看電影？），I wonder how big is this airplane?（這架飛機有多大呢？）。

❸ Are you alright? 你還好嗎？

用於問候人好不好。乍聽之下好像是對方不舒服或是發生什麼事情才會問的問句，不過這句話在外國人口中並不帶有負面的意思，僅是出於關心。就像是 how are you 一樣問候你好嗎？不過 how are you 比較適合用在剛見面時的招呼語，如果已經見過面了或在對談中的話便可以用 are you alright。相同的意思也可以用 Is everything alright?，同樣表示關心，問候一切還好嗎。

❹ I'm good. 我很好（不用了，謝謝）

I'm good 除了用在回答別人的問候之外，也可表示委婉地拒絕別人。像是用餐過後服務生會問 Would you like some tea, coffee, or any desserts?（要來點茶、咖啡或點心嗎？），如果不想要的話就可以說 I'm good, thank you.，這時服務生就會知道你已經飽了、一切都很好，所以不用再上點心了。另外，除了 I'm good 之外，也可以用 I'll pass, thank you.（我就略過點心了，謝謝。）來表示拒絕。

❺ willing to 願意、樂意

表示樂意幫助某人。在服務業中很常會用到的短句，如：She is willing to help others at any time.（她隨時都很樂意幫助他人），當被尋求幫忙的時候可以說，I am willing to help.除了表示願意之外，比起 yes, I can help 更有樂意幫忙的意思。

C ▶ Cabin Crew 空服員　P1 ▶ Passenger1 乘客 1
P2 ▶ Passenger2 乘客 2

P1 ▶ Excuse me, there is someone sitting on my seat. Can you help me?

乘客 1 ▶ 不好意思，有人坐到我的位子了，可以幫我看一下嗎？

C ▶ Can I see your boarding pass please? Oh 20A... yes, you're right, seems like the lady is in the wrong seat.

空服員 ▶ 我可以看一下您的登機證嗎？喔 20 A…對，那位小姐似乎坐錯位子了。

C ▶ Ma'am, can I see your boarding pass, please?

空服員 ▶ 小姐，可以看一下您的登機證嗎？

P2 ▶ Here you are.

乘客 2 ▶ 這是我的登機證。

C▸ Sorry, I'm afraid you are in the wrong seat. Your seat number is 21A, and you're sitting in 20A now.

空服員▸ 不好意思，您恐怕坐錯位子了。您的位子在 21A，您坐到 20A 了。

P2▸ Oh, I'm so sorry. I didn't notice that.

乘客 2▸ 喔對不起，我沒注意到號碼。

C▸ It's alright, no worries at all. It happens sometimes. The numbers on the overhead compartment are way too small.

空服員▸ 沒關係，不用擔心，這有時會發生，行李艙上的數字實在太小了。

P1▸ Thanks a lot!

乘客 1▸ 謝謝你！

✈ 單字解析

❶ boarding pass 登機證

Passengers will get their boarding pass when they check in.

乘客在辦登機手續的時候會拿到登機證。

➤ electronic / mobile / e-boarding pass 電子登機證

❷ seem like 似乎

It seems like she is in a good mood today.

她今天心情看起來很好。

❸ notice　*v.*　注意

I didn't notice that water was leaking in the toilet till I went for shower last night.

我昨天晚上洗澡前才發現浴室在漏水。

❹ hatrack　*n.*　行李艙

Passengers often forget to take their belongings in the hatrack.

乘客常常忘了拿放在行李艙裡的東西。

➤ overhead compartment / hatrack / lockers 行李艙

✈ 常用短句

❶ Here you are. 請（把東西交給對方時）

服務生將餐點交給你時會使用 "here you are", "here you go"，
表示請、在這裏、給你的意思，較為口語的用法。如：Here you
are. This is your happy meal.（來，這是你的快樂餐。）

❷ be afraid that 恐怕、害怕

be afraid of 表示害怕的意思，如：I am afraid of dogs.（我怕
狗）。在這裡的 be afraid that... 類似於 I'm sorry but⋯，表示即
將說出可能會讓對方不滿意的事實或答案，加上 afraid that 可以讓
語氣聽起來委婉一些。如：I'm afraid to tell you that your
application is not approved.（很抱歉，你的申請審核沒有通
過。）

❸ No worries. 不用擔心

no worries「不用擔心」常用在回覆別人道歉的時候。如：Sorry that I was late because of the traffic. / No worries at all. I was enjoying my coffee.（抱歉，因為路上有點塞車所以遲到了／完全不用擔心，我剛好點了杯咖啡喝）。除此之外也可以用在回覆別人答謝的時候，表示「沒關係」，如：Thank you for helping me. / No worries, my pleasure.（謝謝你幫忙／沒關係，我的榮幸）。簡單來說 no worries 照字面翻就是不用煩惱，是很口語的方式表達不會、沒關係、別擔心，當你道謝或道歉的時候得到別人回答 no worries 就是叫你不用煩惱啦、沒什麼好道謝或道歉的意思！

❹ not... at all 完全也不…／不客氣

和 no worries 用法類似，在回覆別人的道謝或致歉時也可以說 not at all 表示不客氣、不會的意思。如：Thanks for waiting. / Not at all.（謝謝你等我／不會）。另外 not at all 當副詞使用時也表示完全不會的意思，用來形容某件事情為完全不會的程度。如：I am not good at sports at all.（我對運動完全沒有概念。）、I didn't sleep at all last night.（我昨天晚上完全沒睡覺。）

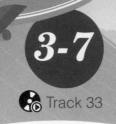

C▸ Cabin Crew 空服員　　**P**▸ Passenger 乘客

(cabin crew announcement) 　　　（空服員廣播中）

C▸ Ladies and gentlemen, the ABC airlines foundation has been devoted to helping children in need around the world. If you would like to donate, you can donate in any currency or online at the foundation website. you can find out more information in your seat pocket. Thank you for your contribution.

空服員▸各位貴賓，ABC 航空基金會致力於幫助世界上需要幫助的孩童們，如果您願意捐獻，您可以使用任何貨幣或是在官網上捐獻。請參考座位前方口袋內的資訊，誠摯感謝您的捐獻。

P▸ (handing a sick bag) Hello, can I hand this to you?

乘客▸（遞嘔吐袋）嗨，這個可以交給你嗎？

C▸ Sorry, what is inside?

空服員▸不好意思請問裡面是什麼？

P ▶ It's the donation for the airline foundation! I heard the announcement that we can donate.

乘客 ▶ 是給基金會的捐款，我剛剛聽到廣播說可以捐獻給孩童。

C ▶ Oh! Thank you so much, but there's another envelope inside the seat pocket, not this one. This is for sickness. But thank you so much, we appreciate it.

空服員 ▶ 哦，非常謝謝您！不過座位口袋裡面有另外一個信封，不是這個，這是嘔吐袋。但還是謝謝您，非常感激！

P ▶ No problem. It is nice to do things like this. I mean helping people around the world, especially your airline spreading love to every place with such ease.

乘客 ▶ 沒什麼啦，幫助世界各地的人真的很棒，尤其你們航空公司可以很簡單就到達各個地方，把愛心散播到各處！

C ▶ Exactly, this is actually what I am doing right now. I collect some clothes etc. and whenever I get African flights, I bring it to them. It might be nothing for us but I know they would love to have it.

空服員 ▶ 沒錯，其實這就是我正在做的，我收集一些衣服等等，只要我有非洲航班我就會帶去給那邊的孩童，對我們來說可能沒什麼，但我知道他們需要，也會很開心。

P ▶ That sounds really amazing!

乘客 ▶ 聽起來真的很棒！

1 招考資訊

2 100%應試準備教戰

3 空服員飛行英語日記

4 附錄

單字解析

❶ foundation *n.* 基金會

This cancer foundation has been found for over 100 years since 1875.

這個癌症基金會從 1875 年起已經成立超過 100 多年了。

➤ since 自從

❷ donate *v.* 捐贈

She donated some clothes to the charity.

她捐了一些衣服給慈善機構。

❸ currency *n.* 貨幣

The change of currency rates is contingent on the circumstance of the economy.

貨幣匯率會視經濟狀況而作改變。

➤ from time to time 有時候

❹ sick bag *n.* 嘔吐袋

There should be sick bags on every seat.

每個座位上都應該會附嘔吐袋。

❺ announcement *n.* 廣播

According to the announcement cabin crew just made, there will be turbulence in 5 minutes.

根據空服員剛剛做的廣播，在五分鐘內會遇到亂流。

➤ turbulence 亂流

常用短句

❶ devote to 致力於

devote to 表示某人致力於某件事物上面，對象可以是興趣、喜歡的人等。to 後面加名詞，如果遇上動詞的話則要將動詞轉成動名詞的形式。如：He has devoted his whole life to charity.（他將他的一生都致力於慈善機構。）

❷ in need 需要

in need（需要）可以有兩個面向的意思，其一是指在危難中、貧困中需要幫助的人們，如：All the donation will go to people in need in Africa.（所有的捐款都會拿去幫助非洲地區貧困的人們。），在這裡的 in need 就是指貧困或在危難中的人們。in need 另一種意思則沒有限定的對象或範圍，如：The roof of this building is in need of repair.（這棟大樓的屋頂需要維修。）

❸ find out 找出、發現

如果你想知道更多資訊的話請參閱椅背口袋的說明。find out 指去發現更多的資訊或確認一件事實，例如：I just found out that I have cancer from the medical report.（我剛才才從健康報告知道我罹患癌症。）、I will find out who was calling all the night.（我會找出晚上到底是誰一直打來。）

❹ I appreciate it. 我很感激、感謝

表示對某人的感謝時，可以說 I appreciate it，比起 thank you 更有感激之意。但要特別小心的是 appreciate 後面只能接事物或子句不能加人。如：I appreciate your kindness.（很感謝你的善解人意。）、I really appreciate that you are willing to help my family.（我真的很感激你能幫助我們家。）。如果後面要接人物的話就用 thank 一詞即可，如：Thank you for your help.（謝謝你的幫忙。）；I appreciate you for your help 是錯誤的用法。

❺ No problem. 不客氣、沒問題

在回覆別人的感謝時，除了可以說 you're welcome 之外，也可以說 no problem 表示「不客氣」。如：Thanks for coming to my speech. / No problem!（謝謝你來聽我的演講／不會！）。而 no problem 除了表示不客氣之外，也可以用在用在回覆別人的道歉。如：Sorry for waiting for so long. / No problem!（不好意思讓妳久等了／沒有問題！）。no problem 是比較口語的講法，用於熟識的朋友間或非正式場合，如果在正式場合比較嚴肅的話建議還是用 You're welcome 表示。

3-8 乘客詢問機上免稅商品

Track 34

C▶ Cabin Crew 空服員　P▶ Passenger 乘客

(During the Flight to New Delhi)　　　（前往新德里的航班上）

(cabin crew announcement)　　　（空服員廣播中）

C▶ Ladies and gentlemen, the cabin crew will be passing through the cabin shortly to take your duty free orders. Please open the duty free magazine for your selection and feel free to contact our cabin crew for more options. Thank you.

空服員▶ 各位貴賓，空服員即將通過機艙販售免稅商品，請瀏覽您的免稅商品雜誌，如果您有任何問題或欲瀏覽更多選項，請不要猶豫洽詢我們的空服人員，謝謝！

P▶ Excuse me, where is the market?

乘客▶ 請問市集在哪裡？

C▶ Market? Which market?

空服員▶ 市集？是什麼市集？

P ▶ The market where you sell things. 　　乘客 ▶ 賣東西的市集。

C ▶ Sorry, I've never been to New Delhi, but I will get more information for you from another crew member, alright? 　　空服員 ▶ 抱歉，我沒去過新德里，但我會向我的同事詢問，可以嗎？

P ▶ No no no, this market! (pointing at the duty free magazine) 　　乘客 ▶ 不是不是，我說的是這個市集。（手指免稅商品雜誌）

C ▶ Ahhh, you mean duty free! Sorry we don't have like an open market for duty free, but I can take your order now. What would you like to buy? 　　空服員 ▶ 哦，你說免稅商品嗎？我們沒有免稅商品的開放市集，不過小姐你有想看哪個商品嗎？我可以幫你找一下。

P ▶ I'd like to buy this watch, but I want to take a look at it first. 　　乘客 ▶ 我想買這支錶，但我想先看一下再決定。

C ▶ Of course, so it's item #1339. Ok ma'am I will come back to you with the item. Would you like to pay by cash or credit card? 　　空服員 ▶ 好啊，所以是編號 1339，好，小姐找一會兒過來找你，你想用現金還是信用卡結帳呢？

P ▶ I don't have that much cash though; can I pay some of it by cash and the rest by credit card?

乘客 ▶ 嗯⋯我現金沒那麼多，我可以付一些現金，剩下的刷卡嗎？

C ▶ Certainly ma'am!

空服員 ▶ 當然！

 單字解析

❶ selection *n.* 選擇

There are thousands of selections for the spices in the spice souk.

香料市集裡有上千種香料供你選擇。

selection 選擇

❷ option *n.* 選項

You can always find an option for food in the airport.

在機場裡你永遠可以找到你想要的食物類型。

❸ market *n.* 市集

There is an open market around the corner open since 1960. Now it has turned to a place more like a shopping area.

轉角那裡有一個從 1960 年就開始營運的開放市集，現在轉型成比較像逛街的地方。

❹ duty-free　*n.*　免稅商品

You can get some duty-free after passing through the customs.

你可以在過海關後買一些免稅商品。

❺ New Delhi　*n.*　新德里（印度首都）

New Delhi is the capital of India.

印度的首都是新德里。

✈ 常用短句

❶ pass through 經過、通過

通過某個地點時可以用 pass through，如：I pass through the park everyday on the way to school.（去上學的途中我都會穿過公園。）和 pass by 不一樣的地方是，pass through 是穿過某個地點，而 pass by 只是經過某個地點。如：I pass by the park everyday on the way to school.（去上學的途中我都會經過公園。），在這句中如果用 pass by 的話就只有經過而不是穿過公園。

❷ take order 點單

在餐飲業很常聽到的一句話，May I take your orders now?（我可以幫你點餐了嗎？），如果當下想點餐了可以說 Yes, please.，但如果還沒決定好，也不要害羞告訴店員晚點再過來。如：Can you come back later?（我還需要一點時間）。除了表示點餐之外，也可以指食物以外的訂單。像是在情境對話中空服員說的 take order 並不是要幫乘客點餐，而是詢問乘客想要買哪些免稅品。而顧客如果要點餐的時候，也一樣可以用 order 這個單字，如：I would like to order now, thank you.（我想點餐了，謝謝）。

❸ feel free 請、儘管、隨意

在日常生活中非常常用到的一句話，也適用在很多場合，表示讓對方放心去做某件事情，通常用在邀請或試著讓對方感到舒適。當有客人來到家裡作客時，可以說 Feel free!（當自己家吧！）；服務業中也很常聽到店員說，Feel free to ask me anything if you have questions.（如果你有什麼問題都可以問我！），想要提供幫助的時候也可以 Feel free to ask for help if you need!（有什麼需要幫助的都可以說！）。

❹ Take a look. 看一下

take a look 表示看一眼某個東西。在買東西的時候很實用的一句話，如：Can I take a look at this necklace please?（我可以看一下這條項鍊嗎？）。而在確定要購買某項物品的時候，也適用 take 這個動詞表示「購買」，如：I will take this one.（我要買這個。）

❺ I will come back to you. 我等一下回來（服務你）。

大家一定有聽過服務生說 "I will come back to you shortly."（我等一下回來。）這句話，表示服務生現在正在忙，或是再接收到顧客的要求之後，正在處理，過一會兒回來。在這裡 come back to you 不僅是回來顧客的身邊，也指 come back to your order。如：Excuse me, can you help me with the form? / Sorry, just a second. I will come back to you.（抱歉可以教我怎麼填這個表格嗎？／等我一下，我一下回來教你）。另外也可以說 "I will be back"、"One second"、"Just a moment" 來表示服務生正在忙，過一下會回來服務你。如果聽到這個請不要吝嗇給服務生一點時間喔！

❻ by credit card / cash 用信用卡／現金付款

Would you like to pay by cash or credit card?（你想要用現金還是信用卡結帳呢？），在結帳時常聽到服務生問的一句話。by 現金或信用卡，表示你付款的方式，非常簡單好懂。

❼ Certainly! 當然、沒有問題

回答別人的請求時，可以用 certainly 表示「沒有問題」、「非常樂意」的意思。除了 certainly 之外，也可以用 absolutely 表示「當然」。如：Can I please have some sugar with the coffee? / Certainly!（我可以要一些糖嗎？／當然！）

C▶ Cabin Crew 空服員　P▶ Passenger 乘客

(On the Flight to Amsterdam)　（前往阿姆斯丹的班機上）

C▶ Duty free! Duty free! Would anyone like duty free items?

空服員▶ 免稅商品！免稅商品！有人要買免稅商品嗎？

P▶ Hi excuse me, how can I buy duty free?

乘客▶ 嗨，請問要怎麼買免稅商品？

C▶ Yes, it's very easy sir. You just need to choose which item you want, and use the little paper inside the duty free magazine to write down the item number and your seat number. Hand it to anyone of our crew and we will come back to you.

空服員▶ 是的先生，很簡單，您只要選好您想要的商品，然後在免稅商品雜誌裡面有表格，寫下商品的代碼跟您的座位號碼，把它交給任何一個我們的同仁就可以了。

P ▸ Cool! Thanks a lot!

乘客 ▸ 我知道了，謝謝！

C ▸ No worries!

空服員 ▸ 不會！

P ▸ Hello, can I give you this? (handing the duty free paper)

乘客 ▸ 哈囉，這個可以給你嗎？（遞免稅商品表格）

C ▸ Of course, Sir! Hold on a second, I will come back to you for the items you wrote down.

空服員 ▸ 可以啊！你等我一下，我去準備你的商品。

P ▸ Cheers!

乘客 ▸ 謝謝！

✈ 單字解析

❶ Amsterdam *n.* 阿姆斯特丹

She went to Amsterdam for two weeks on her vacation.

她放假的時候去了阿姆斯特丹兩個禮拜。

❷ magazine *n.* 雜誌

The record producer used to write music column for a magazine.

那位唱片製作人過去曾在一家雜誌寫音樂專欄。

❸ item number *n.* 商品代碼

Please write down the item number on the paper. I'll track it for you.

請在紙上寫下商品代碼，我幫您查一下。

✈ 常用短句

❶ Anyone would like... ? 有人想要…？

Anyone would like 也可以說成 Would anyone like，如：Anyone would like something to drink? / Would anyone like something to drink?（有人想要喝些東西嗎？）另外還有 Does anyone want 這個說法，如：Does anyone want a coke?（有人想要喝可樂嗎？）不過，這樣的口氣略顯直接，若是用在服務業上，還是以 Anyone would like 這樣的句子，較為客氣、有禮貌。

❷ **How can I... ? 要怎麼…？**

How can I 有「我該如何、我要怎麼」的意思，如：How can I check the status of my visa application?（我要怎麼查詢簽證申請的進度？）另外，how could you (do something)? 則有你怎麼能（做某事）的意思，通常說話者說這句話時，不見得期盼一定要得到對方的回覆。如：How could you do that?（你怎麼能那樣做？）How could you?（你怎麼可以這樣？）

❸ **Hold on a second. 稍等一下**

hold on 表示「等一下」的意思，hold on 後面常常會接 a minute, a second 這些極短暫的時間，但並不是要對方等一分鐘或一秒鐘，只是告訴對方請等一下馬上就會好了。我們在講電話的時候也常會用到 hold on 表示請對方稍等一下將把電話轉給對方要找的人。如：Can I speak to Jane? / Hold on a second.（我找珍／請稍等一下）。hold on 除了「等一下」之外，也有「抓住」、「撐住」的意思。Can you hold on to this string?（你可以抓緊繩子嗎？）在對方遇到艱難狀況的時候，我們也可以用 hold on 鼓勵對方，表示「加油」、「撐住」的意思。如：I know it's a very tough time for you, but please hold on, you will make it through!（我知道你現在的狀況很艱難，但請堅持下去，你會撐過去的！）。

C ▶ Cabin Crew 空服員　P ▶ Passenger 乘客

(On the Flight to Amsterdam)

（前往阿姆斯丹的班機上）

C ▶ Sir, this is your item. For your information, we have a duty free promotion today. If you buy two watches today, you can get 15% off.

空服員 ▶ 先生，這是你的免稅商品。然後跟你說一下，今天我們有免稅商品促銷活動，買兩支手錶可以享八五折優惠。

P ▶ You mean I can get the discount straight away or is it like a coupon for my next purchase?

乘客 ▶ 妳是說我可以直接有折扣，還是像優惠券那樣下次買才有優惠？

C ▶ It's 15% off straight away, sir.

空服員 ▶ 是直接享有八五折優惠。

P ▶ Cool! Sorry can you give me some more time to take a look at another one? I would like to take two!

乘客 ▶ 太棒了，那可以再讓我看一下嗎？我想買兩支。

C ▶ No problem. Take your time!

空服員 ▶ 好啊，沒問題，您慢慢看。

P ▶ Hello, I've decided. I will take this two. Thanks for waiting!

乘客 ▶ 哈囉，我決定好了，我選這兩個！謝謝你等我那麼久。

C ▶ No worries at all! How would you like to pay, by cash or credit card?

空服員 ▶ 不用擔心！你想要付現還是刷卡呢？

P ▶ Do you accept debit cards by any chance?

乘客 ▶ 你們接受提款金融卡嗎？

C ▶ Sorry sir, we only accept credit cards. We do accept quite a few different currencies!

空服員 ▶ 不好意思我們只接受信用卡，但現金的部分我們收滿多貨幣的，你要不要考慮一下？

P ▸ Okay, I will pay by Japanese Yen and Euros, is that alright?

乘客 ▸ 好，那我用日幣跟歐元付可以嗎？

C ▸ Sure! Here you are, and this is your change.

空服員 ▸ 當然！這是你的商品，然後找零。

P ▸ Thank you very much!

乘客 ▸ 謝謝！

單字解析

❶ coupon *n.* 優惠券

My mom likes to collect coupons from every newspaper or magazine.

媽媽喜歡收集報紙或雜誌上的優惠券。

❷ purchase *n.* 購買、交易

Her purchase by the credit card wasn't successful because she didn't validate her card.

她的信用卡交易並沒有成功，因為她還沒有開卡。

➢ validate 使有效

❸ debit card *n.* 提款金融卡

Different from credit card, by debit card, you can only use the amount in your account.

和信用卡不一樣的是，用提款金融卡的話，你只能使用你帳戶裡的額度。

❹ Japanese Yen / Euros *n.* 日幣／歐元

You can exchange both Japanese Yen and Euro in this bank.

在這家銀行你可以換到日幣跟歐元。

✈ 常用短句

❶ For your information. 供你參考／讓你了解一下

在和別人聊天的時候如果提供對方額外的訊息可以說 for your information，這個資訊有可能是對方原本不知道、或是對對方來說是實用的。如：Do you know how can I get to the opera? / Yes, just turn right at the second corner. For your information, it closes at 9 pm. （你知道要怎麼到歌劇院嗎？／第二個轉角右轉，然後歌劇院九點就關了，讓你知道一下）。

❷ get... off 打…折

我們常常可以在國外看到拍賣時店家標示「多少%off」，表示打折的意思。不過和台灣不一樣的是，台灣是直接說打多少折，而國外是說多少%不用錢（off）。如：如果我們說打七折的話，表示三折不用錢，在國外就會標示成「30%off」。另外在店家常見的標示還有 sale（特價）、clearance（清倉拍賣）、yard / garage sale（舊物出清、二手拍賣）等等。

❸ straight away 直接、馬上

straight away 表示「馬上、直接」的意思，也可寫作
straightaway，和 right away、immediately 意思一樣。如：Go
take a shower straightaway when you get home.（回家後立
刻去洗澡。）

❹ Take your time. 你慢慢來、不急

take your time 非常口語、運用的範圍極廣，意指「你慢慢來」、
「不急」的意思。如：Take your time think about it. It is quite
serious.（你慢慢考慮，這件事很嚴肅）。也很常被用在服務業，
比如說客人在看菜單、看商品的時候，店員常會說 take your time
指的就是你慢慢看、不急。

1 招考資訊

2 100%應試準備教戰

3 空服員飛行英語日記

4 附錄

3-11 乘客身體不適

Track 37

C ▶ Cabin Crew 空服員   P ▶ Passenger 乘客

(During The Flight to Taipei)　　　（前往台北的班機上）

P ▶ Sorry, I'm not feeling okay.

乘客 ▶ 抱歉，我不太舒服！

C ▶ Is everything alright? Let me just grab a pen and paper. So how do you feel now?

空服員 ▶ 還好嗎？等等讓我拿個紙筆。您現在感覺怎麼樣？

P ▶ I feel a bit dizzy, weak, and nauseous.

乘客 ▶ 我覺得頭有點暈，然後感覺很虛弱，還有點想吐。

C ▶ Ok, when does this happen?

空服員 ▶ 好，這些症狀是什麼時候開始有的？

P ▸ I think after take-off. I started to feel weird.

乘客 ▸ 起飛之後我就開始覺得有點怪怪的。

C ▸ When was the last time you eat?

空服員 ▸ 你上次吃東西是什麼時候？

P ▸ Around 9 a.m. in the morning.

乘客 ▸ 差不多早上九點。

C ▸ Do you have any history of allergy or diagnosis?

空服員 ▸ 你有過敏或其他疾病的歷史嗎？

P ▸ No.

乘客 ▸ 沒有。

C ▸ Ok. Are you taking any medicine right now?

空服員 ▸ 你近期有在服用任何藥物嗎？

P ▸ No.

乘客 ▸ 沒有。

C ▸ Ok so since the last time you had something to eat, it has been a while. We took off at 1 p.m. now it's 2 p.m., so you haven't eaten for 5 hours.

空服員 ▸ 好，從你上次吃東西已經有一陣子了，我們下午一點起飛，現在是兩點鐘，你大概有五個小時沒吃東西了。

Also, it has been really bumpy while we took up. Maybe that's why you feel nauseous. So I will give you some juice to drink and some crackers to eat first. Let's see if you are getting better. We will be following up with you. And just don't hesitate to call us whenever you need assistance, alright?

另外，因為起飛的時候搖晃很大，所以你可能因為這樣感覺有點噁心。我先給你一些果汁和餅乾填飽肚子，然後我們再看看你有沒有比較好，我們會持續關心你的狀況，如果你有任何需要協助，請儘管告訴我們。

P ▸ Thank you so much.

乘客 ▸ 好，謝謝。

(after some time)

（過了一些時間）

C ▸ Are you feeling better?

空服員 ▸ 你有感覺比較好了嗎？

P ▸ Yes, I feel so much better. Thank you so much!

乘客 ▸ 有，感覺好多了，非常謝謝你。

C ▸ Anytime.

空服員 ▸ 不會喔！

🛩 單字解析

❶ nauseous *adj.* 噁心、想吐的

I feel nauseous after taking the roller coaster.

坐完雲霄飛車之後我覺得很想吐。

❷ dizzy *adj.* 頭暈的

Sometimes you may feel dizzy for not having eaten anything for a long period of time.

有時候，你太久沒吃東西可能會覺得頭暈。

❸ allergy *n.* 過敏

She has seafood allergy since she was little, so she cannot take any seafood at all.

她從小就對海鮮過敏，所以她一點海鮮都不能碰。

❹ diagnosis *n.* 診斷

The diagnosis of my disease was Diabetes.

我的病情診斷結果是我有糖尿病。

❺ bumpy *adj.* 搖晃的

It is quite bumpy when we fly through the sea.

飛機飛過海洋上方的時候很搖晃。

✈ 常用短句

❶ How do you feel? 你感覺怎麼樣？

和 How are you？類似，在打招呼、問候別人的時候我們也可以說 How do you feel today?（你今天怎麼樣呀？）。若是別人不舒服的時候，也可以用 How do you feel？來詢問對方當下的身體狀況。另外，若是 how do you feel 後面加上 about 的話，表示詢問對方「對某件事物的看法」，如：How do you feel about the dishes today?（你覺得今天的晚餐如何？）。

❷ take medicine 服用藥物

服用藥物有專有的動詞 "take" 而不是 "eat"。如：She is taking the medicine for diabetes.（她正在服用糖尿病的藥）。

❸ get better 好轉

用來形容人事物的狀況有逐漸好轉。用在人的部分可以指稱身體狀況或心情，如：He is getting better from the accident.（他已經從車禍的受傷中好轉許多。），如：The condition of his finance is getting better.（他的經濟狀況已經改善許多。）相反地，如果要表示狀況越來越糟糕，則是 get worse，要注意的是不論狀況變好或變壞，get 後面都要加比較級形容詞來形容現在與之前狀況的差別。

❹ follow up 追蹤、跟進

follow up 指的是持續追蹤某件事情的後續狀況，如：Please follow up on the meetings result and let me know.（請持續追蹤開會的結果，並通知我。），在本情境對話中因為乘客不舒服，所以在這裡的 follow up on you 指的是持續了解、關心你的身體狀況。這裡要特別注意的是 follow up 後面不可以直接接代名詞，若是要接代名詞則要加上 on，如：How is the meeting? Please follow up on it!（會議開得怎麼樣？請持續追蹤）。

❺ Do not hesitate to... 不要猶豫做⋯

在提供他人幫忙的時候這句話很好用，和 feel free 很類似，意指告訴別人如果有任何問題不要猶豫、不要擔心聯絡我、儘管告訴我的意思，如：Do not hesitate to tell me if you need something.（你需要什麼的話儘管跟我說。）。這句話也很常被用在履歷中，如：Please do not hesilate to contact me for any further information.（若是需要更多的資訊，請儘管聯絡我。）自傳或履歷通常不會寫得太詳盡，如果主管對你有興趣，想更深入了解你的話，他們可以再聯絡你，因此這句話便做了很好的開場。

3-12 起飛延誤

A ▸ Captain 機長　　P ▸ Passenger 乘客　　C ▸ Cabin Crew 空服員

(Captain's announcement)　　　　　（機長廣播中）

A ▸ Ladies and gentlemen, this is the captain speaking. Just a quick update for you. The delay we are having now is due to traffic control. We are requested to stay at the gate about 10-15 more minutes till further instructions are given. Sorry about the delay, if there is further information we will let you know. Thank you.

機長 ▸ 各位先生女士，這是機長廣播，為大家更新一下現在的狀況。因為交通管制因素，我們被要求待在閘門口大約 10 到 15 分鐘直到有下個指示，很抱歉造成誤點，如果有最新的狀況我們會即時通知您，謝謝。

P ▸ This is taking so long. I have a connecting flight after this. I'm going to be late.

乘客 ▸ 怎麼這麼久，我還有轉機的班機要搭。我會遲到。

C ▶ Yes sir, can I help you?

空服員 ▶ 是的,先生。需要我幫忙嗎?

P ▶ How long is the delay?

乘客 ▶ 飛機還要延誤多久?

C ▶ According to the captain, it will be a 10-15 minutes longer wait at the gate.

空服員 ▶ 根據剛剛機長的廣播,我們還會停留在閘門口大約 10 到 15 分鐘的時間。

P ▶ And what is the reason for that?

乘客 ▶ 為什麼會延誤?

C ▶ Because it's a rush time now, there are a lot of aircraft waiting to take off and we are queuing as well.

空服員 ▶ 因為現在是機場的尖峰時間,很多飛機都在等著起飛,我們也在排隊等起飛中。

P ▶ I have a connecting flight. Do you think I will make it?

乘客 ▶ 我還有轉機的班機要搭,你覺得我搭得上嗎?

C ▶ When is your connecting flight?

空服員 ▶ 您的班機是幾點?

P ▸ It's 3 hours after we land.

乘客 ▸是這班降落後的三小時。

C ▸ I think so sir, because we land much earlier than the scheduled time. Even if you miss the flight, our ground staff will arrange the earliest flight for you to your final destination. No worries.

空服員 ▸ 應該可以,因為我們比表定降落時間提早很多,就算您趕不上,到機場之後,會有我們的地勤人員幫您安排最快的一班飛機,到達您的最終目的地。請不用擔心。

P ▸ What about my luggage?

乘客 ▸那我的行李呢?

C ▸ It will be there at your final destination.

空服員 ▸ 也會一起送到您的最終目的地。

P ▸ I got it. Thank you.

乘客 ▸ 我知道了,謝謝你。

單字解析

❶ update *v.* 更新

Please update your Facebook status. I miss you so much!

拜託請更新你臉書的動態，我好想念你！

❷ instruction *n.* 指示

They followed the instructions on the map to get to the meeting.

他們照著地圖上的指示找到了會議的地點。

❸ connecting flight *n.* 轉機航班

I have a connecting flight to New York from Milan.

我要在米蘭轉機到紐約。

❹ queue *v.* 排隊

We queued for 2 hours to get the ticket for the museum.

我們排了兩個小時買博物館的門票。

❺ scheduled time *n.* 表定時間

According to scheduled departure time, we are supposed to leave 1 hour ago.

根據表定時間，我們一小時前就該起飛了。

✈ 常用短句

❶ due to 由於、因為

表示導致某件事情的原因我們可以用 due to，如：Her absence was due to her mother's sickness.（她缺席是因為她媽媽生病了）。相似的短句還有 because of，如：Because of typhoon, a lot of flights are canceled.（因為颱風的關係，很多航班都取消了。）

❷ requested to 被要求

要求的用法有很多，如：request、ask、require 等，在這裡使用 request 是因為本航班被塔台要求停留在閘門口，屬於較正式且語氣強的用法，通常是對方有權利得到其要求的事項。如：She was requested to stay on her seat until everyone has left.（她被要求留在座位上直到大家都離開了）。相較於 request，ask 為較輕鬆且不強制的語氣，也常用在請求別人的時候，例如：Can I ask for a cup of tea?（我可以要一杯茶嗎？）。而 require 則是用在規定、法律需求方面，例如：We are required to pay tax.（我們必須繳稅）。

❸ according to 根據

根據某人或某資訊管道的說法，可以使用 according to 來表示。如：According to Sean, this event last for 5 days.（根據 Sean 的說法，這個活動為期五天。）；如：According to the plan, we will need to stay at the auditorium until 6 p.m..（根據計畫，我們必須在禮堂待到六點才能走。）要特別注意的是，according to 通常是根據他人的說法，所以不能加上第一人稱代詞，例如：According to me, she will not attend the campaign. 這樣的寫法是錯誤的，可以說 In my opinion, she is not attending the campaign.

❹ make it 做到、達成

make it 表示「達成」、「做到」，是非常口語且使用的範圍很廣，如，可以指成就上的滿足、搭上某交通工具、趕上時間等等。在此對話中乘客說 I will make it 則是第二種用法：成功搭到交通工具。另外，在和某人約定時間時，也可以用 make it 來表示，如：Can you make it at 9:00?（你九點有辦法到嗎？）和 Let's meet at 9.的意思是一樣的。

C▶ Cabin Crew 空服員　　P▶ Passenger 乘客

(On The Flight to Frankfurt)

（前往法蘭克福的班機上）

P▶ Excuse me, can I have a vegetarian meal?

乘客▶請問，我可以點素食餐嗎？

C▶ Yes, sir. Did you order a vegetarian meal before the flight?

空服員▶先生，您有預訂速食餐嗎？

P▶ Do I need to order it? Sorry, I didn't know that, I didn't order anything.

乘客▶哦，我們需要事先預訂喔？我不知道欸，我沒有訂任何東西。

C▶ Yes. If you'd like to order a special meal, you're required to order it while booking the ticket; so

空服員▶是的，如果您想預定特別餐，必須在買票時預定，我們才會事先知

we can prepare it for you on the flight.

道，然後在航班上幫您準備。

P ▶ Is it too late to order now?

乘客 ▶ 現在點還來得及嗎？

C ▶ Unfortunately, it's too late. The vegetarian meal we have on board is for those who have ordered already. However, we do have some fruit and bread, if you don't mind, would you like to have some?

空服員 ▶ 恐怕來不及了，因為班機上的素食餐是給那些有預定特別餐的乘客。不過呢，我們是有一些水果跟麵包，如果您不介意的話，要不要幫您準備一些？

P ▶ Thank you. That would be great!

乘客 ▶ 謝謝，真是太好了！

C ▶ No worries. Just remember next time to order before the flight, so we can prepare it for you sir.

空服員 ▶ 不用擔心，記得下次買票的時候也順便訂素食餐噢，我們才可以提前幫您準備。

P ▶ I will, thank you.

乘客 ▶ 好的，謝謝你！

單字解析

❶ Frankfurt *n.* 法蘭克福（德國一城市）

The European Central Bank is headquartered in Frankfurt.

歐洲中央銀行位於法蘭克福。

❷ vegetarian *adj.* 素食的　*n.* 素食者

He is a vegetarian since he was little.

他從小開始就吃素。

❸ order *v.* 點餐

The last order in this restaurant is 10:30 p.m.

這家餐廳最後點餐的時間是晚上 10:30。

❹ book *v.* 預定

This restaurant is too famous that you need to book it a month before.

這家餐廳太有名了，你必須一個月前就訂位。

❺ prepare *v.* 準備

She prepared everything for the Christmas party.

她準備了聖誕派對要用的所有東西。

✈ 常用短句

❶ unfortunately 不巧、不幸的

在拒絕別人的時候，與其直接說 no，不如使用 unfortunately 吧！
這樣會讓人覺得你不是有心要拒絕，而是很不巧地無法幫上忙。
如：與其說 Sorry, I can't help you now.（抱歉我沒辦法幫你。）
不如說 "Unfortunately, I have few things coming up."（很不
巧的，我還有一些事情要忙。）相較之下，使用 unfortunately 拒
絕別人顯得委婉些。

❷ however 然而

however 用在語句轉折處，表示「然而」、「但是」。如：He
seems to be happy; however, it is not the truth.（他看起來很
開心，但那不是事實。）

相似的用法還有 but, nevertheless 等，同樣表示然而的意思，
如：She is very tired; nevertheless, she went helping her
colleges.（她很累了，然而她還是去幫忙她同事）。

however 也可以作「無論如何」的意思。如：However hard he
tries, he can never win her heart.（無論他多麼努力，也無法擄
獲她的芳心）。

1 招考資訊

2 100%應試準備教戰

3 空服員飛行英語日記

4 附錄

❸ If you don't mind. 你不介意的話

If you don't mind 是一個非常口語、出現率極高並且適用在很多情境的短句，用在請求別人時較委婉的說法，通常也會以問句 Do / Would you mind...?（你介意…嗎？）出現。如：Do you mind if I open the window?（你介意我把窗戶打開嗎？）或是 Can I open the window, if you don't mind?（我可以開窗戶嗎？你不介意的話。）

要注意的是 mind 後面如果加上動詞的話要以動名詞的形式出現，如：Do you mind opening the window?（你介意開一下窗戶嗎？）；如果後面接句子的話則要加上 if，Do you mind if I smoke?（你介意我抽煙嗎？）

下次請求別人的時候不妨用 mind 練習看看喔！

❹ That would be great. 那真是太好了

在餐廳或商店時常會聽到店員問你需不需要這個或那個，我們除了回答 yes 跟 no 之外，更好的方法是說 That would be great!（那真是再好不過了！）。如：Would you like some milk with the tea?（請問茶要加牛奶嗎？）

除了可以說 yes 之外，我們也可以說 That would be great!（那真是太好了！）來表示好，而其中的 great 也可以用其他形容詞替代，如：fantastic, amazing, awesome, nice 等等，聽起來也更加愉悅及有禮貌。

而與其直接說 no，還有其他的替代說法聽起來比較委婉，如：I will skip that.（我就略過它了），skip 略過表示「不需要」的意思；也可以說 I'm good.（我很好），表示我很好，所以已經不需要其他餐點（或服務）了。

C▶ Cabin Crew 空服員　P▶ Passenger 乘客

(On the Flight to Paris)　　　　　（前往巴黎的班機上）

(Cabin Crew making announcement)　　（空服員廣播中）

C▶ Ladies and gentlemen, as we are passing through an area of turbulence, please return to your seat, fasten your seatbelt, and refrain from using the lavatories at this time. Thanks for your cooperation.

空服員▶ 各位先生女士，由於我們現在通過一段亂流，請你返回到座位上繫好安全帶，並且暫時不要使用廁所。謝謝您的合作。

C▶ Sir, please return to your seat and fasten your seatbelt.

空服員▶ 先生，請您回到座位上並繫好安全帶。

P▶ II'll just use the lavatory just for 2 minutes. I've been waiting for so long.

乘客▶ 我上一下廁所兩分鐘就好了，我已經排很久了。

C▸ Sorry sir, as the captain has switched on the seatbelt sign, you have to go back to your seat and fasten your seatbelt right now. You can use it when the seatbelt sign is off.

空服員▸ 抱歉先生，由於機長開啟安全帶指示燈，你現在必須返回座位，並繫上安全帶，您可以在安全帶指示燈熄滅後再來上廁所。

P▸ Ok. Can I have some tea please?

乘客▸ 好吧。那我可以要一杯茶嗎？

C▸ I'm sorry sir, because it is quite bumpy now, we have stopped serving tea coffee at this time. If you would like to wait, I will come back to you when it gets better.

空服員▸ 抱歉，因為現在搖晃太大，所以我們暫停茶跟咖啡的服務，你願意等的話，等情況比較好一點我在幫你送。

P▸ Ok, thanks.

乘客▸ 好，謝謝！

P▸ Sorry, I feel like vomiting. Where is the airsickness bag?

乘客▸ 抱歉，我覺得我快吐了，嘔吐袋在哪裡？

C▸ The airsick bag is in the seat pocket in front of you.

空服員▸ 在你前方的椅背口袋內。

1 招考資訊

2 100%應試準備教戰

3 空服員飛行英語日記

4 附錄

✈ 單字解析

❶ turbulence　*n.*　亂流

Some turbulence is predictable but some are not.

有些亂流可以預測，但是有些則不行。

❷ serve　*v.*　服務

He served some extra tea for the lady who is really fond of it.

他多送了一些茶給那位喜歡茶的女士。

❸ vomit　*v.*　嘔吐

The little boy at the last row vomited after we landed.

坐在最後一排的小男孩在飛機降落後吐了。

❹ cooperation　*n.*　合作

Cooperation is really important especially in team activity.

在團隊活動中合作顯得特別重要。

✈ 常用短句

❶ refrain from 抑制、克制、避免

refrain 表「抑制、避免」做某項行為，通常與 from 連用，並且後面要接上動名詞。如：Please refrain from shouting in the library.（在圖書館內請避免喧嘩。）

❷ at this time 此時

at this time 是此時的意思，在文中指的此時就是亂流發生的這段時間。如：It is really not nice to ask her out at this time. She needs some time to recover.（此時約她出來真的不是時候，她需要一些時間康復。）

❸ switch on 打開…開關

switch on 表示「打開某種電器或電子產品的開關」，除了 switch on / off 外也可用 turn on / off 來表示。因為中文的關係，我們常會不小心講成 open the light、open your computer 等，要特別小心如果是打開電子／器產品的話要用動詞 switch / turn on 喔。

❹ feel like 想要

除了可用 want to 表示「想要」之外，feel like 也是外國人很常用來表示「想要」的短句。如：I feel like taking a shower.（我想要洗個澡。）也可使用 feel like 告訴餐廳店員想點什麼，如：I feel like having an ice cream.（我想要吃冰淇淋。）而 feel like 除了「想要」的意思外，也可表示某事物對人或某人對某事的感覺。如：It feels like rain.（好像要下雨了。）；She feels like part of the family after living with her friend for 2 months.（在她朋友家住了兩個月之後，她感覺像是她們的家人了。）

C ▶ Cabin Crew 空服員　P ▶ Passenger 乘客

(Cabin Crew announcement)　（空服員廣播）

C ▶ Ladies and gentlemen, as we are passing through an area of rough air, please remain seated with your seatbelt fastened and refrain from using the lavatories at this time.

空服員 ▶ 各位乘客，由於我們正穿越一段不穩定的氣流，請您留在座位上繫好安全帶，並暫時不要使用廁所。

C ▶ Hello sir, would you like to have chicken with potato or beef with rice for dinner?

空服員 ▶ 哈囉先生，您晚餐要吃雞肉配馬鈴薯，還是牛肉配飯呢？

P ▶ I'll take the chicken, thanks.

乘客 ▶ 雞肉好了，謝謝。

C ▶ Anything to drink?

空服員 ▶ 要喝什麼嗎？

P ▶ Can I have some tea please?

乘客 ▶ 可以給我杯茶嗎？

C▸ Sure, would you like some milk or sugar with it?

空服員▸ 要加牛奶或糖嗎？

P▸ Just some milk, thanks.

乘客▸加一些牛奶好了。

C▸ There you go.

空服員▸ 來，給您。

(Cabin Crew announcement)

（空服員廣播）

C▸ Ladies and gentlemen, as we are passing through an area of rough air, we will not offer tea or coffee services for safety reasons. We apologize for the inconvenience.

空服員▸ 各位乘客，由於我們正穿越一段不穩定的氣流，考量安全問題，我們會暫時取消茶和咖啡的服務，造成您的不方便深感抱歉。

P▸ Can I have some coffee please?

乘客▸可以給我一杯咖啡嗎？

C▸ Sorry sir it's too bumpy now, so we are not offering hot beverage service for a while.

空服員▸ 不好意思，因為現在太搖晃了，所以我們暫時停止咖啡跟茶的服務。

P▸ It's alright.

乘客▸沒問題。

1 招考資訊

2 100%應試準備教戰

3 空服員飛行英語日記

4 附錄

✈ 單字解析

❶ rough air *n.* 不穩定氣流

We are passing through an area go rough air, please sit down.

請坐下，我們正穿越一段不穩定的氣流。

❷ remain *v.* 保持

She remains her figure very well. You can't tell she's already 40.

她身材保持得很好，你看不出來她有 40 歲。

❸ inconvenience *n.* 不方便

We apologize for the inconvenience we caused.

造成您的不方便我們深感抱歉。

✈ 常用短句

❶ as... 因為、由於

as 做「因為、由於」的意思時，可以放句首或句中。如：As we have been to Paris, we are familiar with their public transportation.（由於我們去過巴黎，所以我們對它的大眾運輸工具頗熟悉。）Linda has no idea how to get to station as she just moves in the town.（琳達不知道怎麼去車站，因為她才剛搬進小鎮。）

❷ remain seated 留在座位上

連綴動詞 remain 後面要接形容詞。remain 有「保持、保留」的意思，通常用於人或物停留在某個地方，或是保持在一個狀態。如：Please remain seated with your seatbelt fastened.（請您留在座位上並繫好安全帶。）另一個字 maintain，有「保持、維持」的意思，多用於表示人或物持續存在，或保持在一定的狀態沒有減緩。如：They maintain their friendship for twenty years.（他們維持了二十年的友誼。）

3-16 亂流：空服員請坐下

Track 42

U▶ Purser 座艙長　C▶ Cabin 空服員　P▶ Passenger 乘客

(Purser announcement)　　　　　　　（空服員廣播）

U▶ Cabin Crew take your seat.　　　座艙長▶ 空服員請坐下。

U▶ Once again ladies and gentlemen, as we are passing through turbulence, we request all passengers remain seated and fasten your seatbelt. Cabin crew will be taking their seats for safety reasons. We will stop service for a while. Thanks for your understanding.

座艙長▶ 各位乘客，再一次，由於我們現在正通過亂流，請各位乘客留在座位上，繫好安全帶。由於安全考量，空服員會在椅子上坐著，我們將暫停餐飲服務，謝謝您的諒解。

(after one hour)　　　　　　　　　（一小時之後）

C ▸ Hello sorry for waiting, would you like chicken or beef?

空服員 ▸ 哈囉，抱歉久等了，請問您要雞肉還是牛肉？

P ▸ No problem at all. I will have the chicken please. It's not an easy job right. It is bumpy, but you guys still have to do the service. I always get scared when there is turbulence.

乘客 ▸ 完全沒有關係，我吃雞肉好了。這個工作不簡單對吧，這麼搖晃還要做餐飲服務。每次亂流的時候我都超害怕的。

C ▸ Yeah, sometimes! Sometimes I feel like my world is spinning around when the aircraft is turning. Anyway, bon appetite!

空服員 ▸ 對啊有時候，有時候飛機在轉向的時候，我覺得我的天花板在天懸地轉。總之，用餐愉快！

P ▸ Cheers!

乘客 ▸ 謝謝！

✈ 單字解析

❶ request *v.* 要求

She was requested to hand in the report by next week.

她被要求下禮拜要交報告。

❷ understanding *n.* 諒解

Thanks for your understanding. I'm sorry for being late.

很抱歉遲到了，謝謝你的諒解。

✈ 常用短句

❶ Cabin crew take your seat! 空服員請坐下！

在飛機上遇到的亂流有大小之分，也有可預期和不可預期的亂流。通常安全帶指示燈亮起的時候，就表示即將或正在通過亂流，以提醒乘客不要到處走動，要回位子上坐好並繫上安全帶。在很多情況下，亂流的程度可能大到無法做熱飲的服務，因為杯子或茶壺內的熱飲會因為晃動而灑出，不光是影響乘客和服務的空服員，在廚房準備熱飲的空服員也有可能因此而燙傷。更嚴重的亂流是連站都站不穩、東西到處飛的情況，這種時候也顧不得服務了，此時會聽到座艙長或機師廣播叫空服員立刻坐下，以免發生不必要的傷害。在這裡的 Cabin crew take your seat 就是這種狀況。

❷ **Sorry for waiting. 不好意思久等了。**

Sorry for waiting 可以適用在很多情境，除了用在餐飲服務上菜的時候之外，也可以用在講電話的時候，比如轉線到其他部門、轉接給其他人的時候，剛接起電話時我們就可以說 "Sorry for waiting."。另外，和別人約會時如果比較晚到，也可以在到的時候先說這句，讓別人等待的心情和緩下來。總之，在讓對方等待的不管何種情況下，這句話都可以派上用場喔！

❸ **spin around 旋轉**

spin around 字面上的意思就是旋轉，可以用來表示當你不舒服覺得天玄地轉的時候，如：I'm really not feeling well. I feel like the ceiling is spinning around.（我真的不太舒服，我覺得天花板在旋轉。）也可以用在事物真的在旋轉的當下，如：The carousel is spinning around with lights. I love it!（旋轉木馬帶著燈泡在旋轉，我很喜歡！）。另一個層面的意思可以表示迷戀某人，如：You spin me around.（你讓我迷戀得團團轉。）

❹ **Bon appetite! 用餐愉快**

法國人在用餐前會說 Bon appetite，表示祝人用餐愉快，而這個用法已經不侷限於法國人在使用而已，很多外國人在用餐前也會說 Bon appetite!意思就等同於 Enjoy your meal!一樣。因此下次我們除了可以說 Enjoy your meal 之外，又多了一個講法噢！

3-17 乘客在廁所按服務鈴

Track 43

C ▶ Cabin Crew 空服員　P ▶ Passenger 乘客

(On the Flight to London)	（前往倫敦的班機上）
[DING] (toilet call bell)	〔叮〕（廁所服務鈴響）
C ▶ (knocking on the toilet door) Excuse me, ma'am, is everything alright?	空服員 ▶（敲廁所門）小姐，您沒事吧？
P ▶ What???	乘客 ▶ 什麼？
C ▶ I believed you pressed the lavatory assistance button. Are you alright?	空服員 ▶ 你按了廁所的服務鈴，你還好嗎？
P ▶ Ooops! That was a mistake. I intended to flush the toilet. Sorry about that!	乘客 ▶ 噢！我按錯了抱歉，我本來是要沖水的。

C▸ No worries. Can you see there is a blue button bigger than the lavatory assistance call button? That one is the flush button!

空服員▸ 沒關係，你有看到一個比廁所服務鈴還大顆的藍色按鈕嗎？那個是沖水按鈕。

P▸ Oh, I see. By the way, do you have any sanitary items for women here?

乘客▸ 哦！我看到了，對了！你們廁所有女性衛生用品嗎？

C▸ Yes we do. Just there in the little drawer next to the mirror.

空服員▸ 有喔，在鏡子旁邊的抽屜裡。

P▸ Ahh, I found them! Thank you so much!

乘客▸ 我找到了！謝謝。

C▸ No problem.

空服員▸ 不客氣。

✈ 單字解析

❶ press *v.* 按壓

Press the button on the left; it's the switch for the lights.

請按左邊那個按鈕,那是電燈的開關。

➤ switch 開關

❷ call bell *n.* 服務鈴

Please don't play with the call bell, or we won't know if there is an emergency.

請不要玩服務鈴,不然有緊急狀況的時候我們會不知道。

❸ flush *n.* 沖水鈕

There should be a flush near the toilet bowl.

沖水鈕應該會在馬桶附近。

➤ toilet bowl 馬桶

❹ sanitary items *n.* 女性衛生用品

You can ask for sanitary items from the front desk.

你可以向櫃台詢問女性衛生用品。

❺ drawer *n.* 抽屜

There are three drawers by my desk.

我的書桌有三個抽屜。

✈ 常用短句

❶ by the way 順道一提

by the way 表示「順道一提」、「對了」的意思，是非常生活化的用語，可以用在某人在談話中想從 A 話題轉成 B 話題時候使用，通常放在句子的開頭並接續著想要講的話題。例如：By the way, have you seen Brian lately? I haven't seen him for a long time.（對了，你最近有看到布萊恩嗎？我有好一陣子沒見到他了。）除了 by the way 之外，in passing 也可以表示順便的意思，She mentioned in passing that she passed the exam.（她提到她通過考試的事。）

1 招考資訊

2 100％應試準備教戰

3 空服員飛行英語日記

4 附錄

C ▶ Cabin Crew 空服員　P1 ▶ Passenger1 乘客 1

P2 ▶ Passenger2 乘客 2　P3 ▶ Passenger3 乘客 3

(On the Flight to London)　　　　　（前往倫敦的班機上）

C ▶ Hello Sir, would you care for a drink?　　　空服員 ▶ 哈囉先生，請問要喝點飲料嗎？

P1 ▶ What kind of drinks do you have?　　　乘客 1 ▶ 你們有什麼樣的飲料？

C ▶ We have juices, water, soft drinks, wine, beer, sparkling water and so on. Which one do you prefer?　　　空服員 ▶ 我們有果汁、水、汽水、酒、啤酒、氣泡水等等，您想要喝哪種？

P1 ▶ Do you have the nonalcoholic beer?　　　乘客 1 ▶ 你們有無酒精的啤酒嗎？

C▸ Sorry, Sir. We don't have that on board. But we do have some options for regular ones like Heineken or Budweiser...

空服員▸ 不好意思我們飛機上沒有欸，但我們有一般的啤酒像是海尼根、百威…

P1▸ I'll take a Heineken, please.

乘客 1▸ 請給我海尼根。

C▸ Absolutely Sir.

空服員▸ 沒問題。

C▸ Hello Sir, any drinks for you?

空服員▸ 哈囉先生，要喝些什麼嗎？

P2▸ Yes, please. Do you have some fizzy drinks?

乘客 2▸ 你們有氣泡飲料嗎？

C▸ Yes, we have soft drinks like coke, sprite, pepsi...

空服員▸ 有啊，像是可樂、雪碧、百事可樂…

P2▸ May I have coke with lots of ice, please?

乘客 2▸ 可以給我一杯可樂，加很多冰塊嗎？

C▸ Of course.

空服員▸ 沒問題。

C ▸ Hello ladies, would you like to have some drinks?

空服員 ▸ 哈囉小姐，要喝點飲料嗎？

P3 ▸ That would be great! May I please have some coffee?

乘客 3 ▸ 太好了，可以給我一些咖啡嗎？

C ▸ Sure, any milk or sugar with your coffee?

空服員 ▸ 當然，需要加糖跟牛奶嗎？

P3 ▸ Do you have sweetener?

乘客 3 ▸ 你們有糖精嗎？

C ▸ Yes we do. Here you are.

空服員 ▸ 有的，來這給你。

P3 ▸ Cheers!

乘客 3 ▸ 謝謝！

單字解析

❶ nonalcoholic beer *n.* 無酒精啤酒

If you cannot take alcohol you may try the nonalcoholic beer.

如果你不能喝酒，你可以試試看無酒精的啤酒。

❷ option *n.* 選擇

You have two options for the dinner, chicken with potatoes or fish with rice.

晚餐你有兩種選擇，雞肉搭配馬鈴薯，或是魚搭配米飯。

❸ fizzy *adj.* 有氣泡的

This wine is slightly sweet and fizzy.

這瓶酒微甜而且有氣泡。

❹ sweetener *n.* 甜味劑

Some people prefer sweetener because it has lower calories than regular sugar.

有些人喜歡甜味劑，因為它的熱量比一般糖還要低。

✈ 常用短句

❶ Would you care for... ? 請問需要…嗎？

care for 表示「想要」、「希望」的意思，Would you care for something?是在用於詢問他人對於某項物品是否需要、想要，和 would you like something 是一樣的意思，在餐廳有時也會聽到服務生這樣問你。例如：Would you care for another drink?（請問還需要加點飲料嗎？）。另外 care for 也能當成「喜愛」的意思，Do you care for that novel?（你喜歡那本小說嗎？）。

❷ and so on 等等的

在舉例時如果想列舉的東西太多，可以以 and so on 來表示「等等」的意思。例如：There are lots of fruits on the table like apple, mandarin, strawberries, and so on. Just help yourself!（桌上有頻果、橘子、草莓等等的，請不要客氣！）和 and so on 相近意思的 and so forth 也可以在列舉事物時表示「等等」。例如：For your minor study, you can choose Japanese, French, Spanish and so forth.（你的第二學習外語可以選擇日文、法文、西班牙文等等）。

❸ Absolutely! 當然！

absolutely 表示當然的意思，可以使用在答覆別人的請求時。例如：Can I have some water? Absolutely!（可以給我一些水嗎？當然！）。除了 absolutely 之外，of course、certainly、sure、definitely、indeed 等都可以代替 yes 回覆別人的請求。

❹ take... 點（餐）⋯

take 這個動詞除了表示「拿」、「承擔」、「吃藥」⋯⋯之外，take 常常也被用在點餐的時候。例如店員問你要點什麼餐，你可以說 I will take a cheese burger.（我要一個起司漢堡。），和店員幫客人點餐一樣用 take，take order 表示幫客人點餐。例如：I will come back and take your order. Take your time!（我等下回來幫你點餐，你慢慢看！）。

3-19 乘客攜帶嬰兒同行

Track 45

C ▸ Cabin Crew 空服員　P ▸ Passenger 乘客

(On the Flight to Hong Kong)　（前往香港的班機上）

P ▸ Hi excuse me, I'm sorry to bother you.

乘客 ▸ 嗨不好意思，打擾你了。

C ▸ It's alright! How can I help you?

空服員 ▸ 不會啊！需要幫忙嗎？

P ▸ Is it possible to have some milk for my baby?

乘客 ▸ 你們這邊有嬰兒喝的牛奶嗎？

C ▸ Sure! Would you like the regular one or the baby milk?

空服員 ▸ 當然，您要一般鮮奶還是嬰兒牛奶？

P ▸ I'll take the baby milk. Thank you so much. Do you also have diapers on board? Sorry, I just lost my bag at the airport which I put all the baby stuff inside. I was wondering if I could take some more just in case.

乘客 ▸ 可以給我嬰兒牛奶嗎？謝謝。對了，你們有尿布嗎？不好意思我剛在機場掉了我的包包，我全部的嬰兒用品都在裡面，我可以拿多一點嗎？以防萬一。

C ▸ Oh, I feel sorry for you. Are you traveling alone?

空服員 ▸ 噢，我感到很抱歉，你自己一個人嗎？

P ▸ Unfortunately, yes, I am. But it's fine, I am going to meet my husband in Hong Kong. He's working there.

乘客 ▸ 對啊，我跟小孩而已，但我要去香港見我老公，他在那邊工作。

C ▸ No problem at all! Just tell me what else you need. Would you like to have some baby food as well?

空服員 ▸ 沒問題！儘管告訴我您還需要什麼，需不需要嬰兒食物？

P ▸ That would be so nice. Thank you so much. By the way, do you know if I can get a baby trolley at the gate?

乘客 ▸ 好啊，真的很謝謝你。對了，你知道我是否可以在登機門拿到我的嬰兒推車嗎？

C▸ There will be a trolley at the gate for you to borrow, but if you checked in your trolley, you will get it at the carousel.

空服員▸ 登機門那邊有嬰兒車可以借，不過你的嬰兒車如果已經寄行李了的話，要到行李輸送帶那邊領取。

P▸ Cool. Thank you so much. You are so kind!

乘客▸ 我知道了，謝謝你！

C▸ It's nothing!

空服員▸ 不會，這沒什麼。

單字解析

❶ diaper *n.* 尿布

It's time to change his diaper. I smell something.

該幫他換尿布了，已經有味道了。

➤ it's time to 是時候⋯

❷ trolley *n.* 嬰兒推車

You can check in the trolley as well, no need to worry.

你可以託運嬰兒推車，不用擔心。

❸ carousel *n.* 行李輸送帶

There are so many people waiting in front of the carousel. It took me half an hour to get my luggage.

行李輸送帶前面很多人在等行李，我等了半小時才拿到行李。

❹ checked in 托運（行李）

Please make sure you don't have lithium battery in your checked in baggage.

請確認托運行李裡面沒有鋰電池。

常用短句

❶ I'm sorry to bother you. 不好意思打擾你、麻煩你

bother 是打擾、麻煩的意思，sorry to bother you 表示抱歉耽擱到你的時間了，和 excuse me 意思相近，可以用在麻煩別人、打斷別人的時候會顯得較有禮貌。如：Sorry to bother you, do you mind I sit here?（不好意思打擾到你，我可以坐這嗎？）。

No bother（不麻煩）也可以用在回覆別人道謝的時候，表示一點都不麻煩、不用客氣的意思。如：Thank you so much for dropping me home! / No bother!（謝謝你載我回家／不用客氣！）

❷ Is it possible...? 可以／有可能…嗎？

possible 是合理的、可能的，Is it possible to 做某件事、Is it possible for you to 做某件事，表示請求對方做某件事、某件事發生的機率。如：Is it possible to have some water?（有機會跟你要杯水嗎？）這種問法並不是真的要問事件的機率有多大，而是一種請求的用法，類似於 Can I...？

❸ in case 以防萬一

in case 以防萬一，後面接子句，也可以直接以 Just in case. 為一個句子接在後面，如果用 in case of 表示的話後面則要接上名詞。如：Bring an umbrella with you in case it rains. / Bring an umbrella with you. Just in case! / Bring an umbrella with you in case of rain.（帶著傘吧，以免下雨！）

❹ I feel sorry for you. 我感到抱歉

sorry 表抱歉，但在這邊並不是因為做錯了什麼事而道歉。在這裡的 sorry 是用來表示同情的意思，比方說聽到對方的遭遇而表示憐憫、感到抱歉。同樣的用法還有 I feel sorry for you. / I am sorry about that. / I'm sorry 都可以用來安慰對方。如：I just lost my wallet, and all of my cards are inside. / I feel sorry for you. （我錢包掉了，我全部的卡都在裡面／我感到很抱歉）。

3-20　乘客座位螢幕故障

 Track 46

C ▶ Cabin Crew 空服員　P ▶ Passenger 乘客

(On the Flight to Vienna)　　　　　（前往維也納的班機上）

P ▶ Hi excuse me, my screen is not working.

乘客 ▶ 嗨不好意思，我的螢幕壞了。

C ▶ It isn't? Let me check. Oh, it seems like it's stuck here. I will reset your screen, but it might take a few minutes!

空服員 ▶ 是嗎？我看看。看起來它是當機了，我幫您重新啟動這台電視，但需要花上一些時間喔！

P ▶ It's alright.

乘客 ▶ 沒有關係。

C ▶ In the meantime, please do not touch the screen or the hand control. Let's just let it run through again.

空服員 ▶ 在它重開機的期間，請不要觸碰螢幕或是遙控器，就讓它自己重新開機。

P ▸ Sure.

乘客 ▸ 好的。

(after 15 minutes)

（15 分鐘後）

C ▸ Is it working now?

空服員 ▸ 可以看了嗎？

P ▸ Yes it is! Thank you! By the way, do you have any Spanish movies?

乘客 ▸ 可以了！謝謝！對了，你們有西班牙的電影嗎？

C ▸ Do you mean movies with Spanish subtitles or Spanish movies?

空服員 ▸ 您是說有西班牙字幕的電影，還是西班牙電影？

P ▸ Spanish movies. But it will be fine with the Spanish subtitles if you don't have any Spanish ones.

乘客 ▸ 西班牙電影，但有西班牙字幕的電影也可以，如果你沒有西班牙電影的話。

C ▸ Yes we do have some Spanish movies. You can check on the movies list. Otherwise, you can click on the "SUBTITLES" to see if there is a subtitle for a movie movie.

空服員 ▸ 我們有一些西班牙電影，您可以在電影清單上找，不然，您也可以在電影裡頭按「字幕」選項，看看有沒有西班牙字幕。

✈ 單字解析

❶ stuck　*v.*　卡住、當機

My computer got stuck. Can you help me?

我的電腦當機了。你可以幫忙嗎?

❷ reset　*v.*　重新設定、重開機

I will reset your computer. Let's see if it works.

我幫你重新設定電腦,看會不會有用。

❸ Spanish　*adj.*　西班牙文的　*n.*　西班牙文

She has been learning Spanish for 2 years. She can speak it fluently now.

她學西班牙文兩年了,現在可以講得很流利。

❹ subtitles　*n.*　字幕

Most of the TV shows in Taiwan have subtitles.

台灣大部份的電視節目都有字幕。

🛫 常用短句

❶ in the meantime 此時

in the meantime 表示在兩個事件間的時間，或是現在到某個事件發生的期間。如：She goes to work from 9am to 5pm, in the meantime, her baby is taking care by her mother.（她從早上九點工作到下午五點，這期間她的小孩由媽媽照顧。）at the same time 指的是事情在同一時間發生，例如：I was having lunch and studying at the same time.（我邊吃午餐邊唸書。）

❷ You mean... 你指的是⋯

在沒有聽清楚對方說什麼、或是確認對方的意思時除了可以說 Pardon?、Excuse me?、Sorry?之外，我們也可以直接將對方的意思再問一次對方做確認，而在這前面可以加上 You mean... 也就是「你指的是⋯嗎？／你說的是⋯意思嗎？」。如：How's the weather in Taiwan? / You mean average or in a specific season?（台灣的天氣怎麼樣？／你是說整體來說，還是特定的季節？）。

❸ otherwise 否則

otherwise 有除此之外、否則的意思，這裡當「否則」用，如：Hurry up, otherwise you're going to be late.（快點，不然你要遲到了），其中 otherwise 也可以用 if not 替代，同樣也代表否則的意思。例如：Listen to him, if not, you will be in trouble.（聽他的話不然你會有麻煩。）

3-21 乘客睡在地上

Track 47

C ▶ Cabin Crew 空服員　　P ▶ Passenger 乘客

(On the Flight to Vienna)　　　　　　（前往維也納的班機上）

C ▶ Sorry sir, you cannot sleep here.　　空服員 ▶ 先生您不能躺在這裡。

P ▶ Where else can I sleep?　　乘客 ▶ 不然我要在哪裡睡覺？

C ▶ In your seat.　　空服員 ▶ 在您的位子上。

P ▶ But my seat is not big enough.　　乘客 ▶ 我的位子不夠大。

C ▶ You can upgrade to business class to have a bigger seat if you want. Let me double-check the upgrade price for you.　　空服員 ▶ 如果您想要的話，您可以升級到商務艙，那裡有很大的座位。讓我幫您確認升等的價錢。

P ▸ I don't want to upgrade. Why can't I sleep here?

乘客 ▸ 我不想要升等，為什麼我不能睡這裡？

C ▸ It's about safety sir. Passengers are not allowed to sleep on the floor. If you want to stretch, you can walk around the aircraft when the seatbelt sign is off.

空服員 ▸ 這是關於你的安全，乘客是禁止躺在地上的。如果你想要伸展一下的話，你可以在安全帶指示燈沒亮的時候在飛機上走動。

P ▸ Don't you have a place to sleep on board?

乘客 ▸ 你們不是有可以躺著睡覺的地方嗎？

C ▸ That is for crew rest sir. Passengers are not allowed to enter. Do you want me to check the upgrade price?

空服員 ▸ 那是機組人員的休息間，乘客禁止進入。需要幫您確認一下升等的價錢嗎？

P ▸ It's fine. I'll go back to my seat.

乘客 ▸ 不用了，我回去我的座位。

C ▸ Thank you very much, sir.

空服員 ▸ 非常謝謝您喔！

✈ 單字解析

❶ upgrade *n.* 升等、升級

You can upgrade your card by paying 100 more dollars every month.

你可以每個月多繳一百塊升級卡片。

❷ business class *n.* 商務艙

To save travelling expenses, she didn't take business class to Japan.

為了節省旅費，她沒搭商務艙去日本。

❸ double-check 再次確認

Please double-check your luggage to see if there're any dangerous items.

請再次確認你的包包裡有沒有危險物品。

❹ stretch *n.* 伸展

She stretched her body after a long ride.

在很長的車程後，她伸展她的身體。

✈ 常用短句

❶ allowed to 允許

allowed to 允許，通常以被動的語態出現，如：You are not allowed to carry more than 100ml of liquid on board.（上飛機不能攜帶超過 100ml 的液體）。和 permit 以及 let 相比的話，permit 用在較正式的場合、偏向「許可」的意思，如：She is permitted by the government to sell here on the street.（她被政府許可可以在這裡販售東西。而 let 比較偏向於生活上、沒有法律效力的許可，如：She let her children play games for an hour.（她讓她的小孩玩電動一小時。）

❷ it's about... 關於…

說明一項規定是因為考量到什麼因素，可以使用 it's about...這個句子。如：It's about your safety. Please don't leave your seat.（這是為了您的安全，請您別離開座位。）另外，about 表示「關於」時，我們可以拿來形容比較一般性、通俗性的事物，如：an article about astronomy 指的是有可能是給一般大眾閱讀的天文學文章，但如果是 an article on astronomy 就偏向是學術性的文章。

3-22　奧客-1

🎧 Track 48

C1 ▸ **Cabin Crew 1 空服員1**　C2 ▸ **Cabin Crew2 空服員 2**
C3 ▸ **Cabin Crew 1 空服員3**　P ▸ **Passenger 乘客**

[Ding]	〔叮！〕
(call bell rings)	（服務鈴響）
C1 ▸ Hello sir, how can I help you?	空服員1▸ 嗨先生，需要幫忙嗎？
P ▸ Can I get whiskey with coke and ice?	乘客 ▸可以給我一杯威士忌加可樂跟冰嗎？
C1 ▸ Sure, just a second! I'll come back to you.	空服員1▸ 好的，我一會兒回來。
P ▸ Cheers!	乘客 ▸謝謝。

C1 ▶ There you go sir, whiskey with coke.

空服員1 ▶ 先生你的威士忌加可樂。

P ▶ Thanks a lot!

乘客 ▶ 謝啦！

[Ding]

〔叮！〕

(call bell rings)

（服務鈴響）

C1 ▶ Hello, can I help you?

空服員1 ▶ ：哈囉～需要幫忙嗎？

P ▶ Whiskey! Whiskey!

乘客 ▶ 威士忌！威士忌！

C1 ▶ You mean you want a drink sir?

空服員1 ▶ 先生你是說你想要一杯飲料嗎？

P ▶ Bring me whiskey!

乘客 ▶ 給我威士忌！

C1 ▶ I'll be right back. Just a second, sir.

空服員1 ▶ 我一會兒回來。

🛩 單字解析

❶ ding   *n.*   鐘聲

That little girl is annoyed at the ding sound.

那個小女孩被叮噹聲惹毛。

❷ whiskey   *n.*   威士忌

Whiskey with coke is his favorite drink. He has it whenever we're out.

威士忌加可樂是他最喜歡的飲料，他每次都點這個。

🛩 常用短句

❶ just a second 稍等一下

表示「稍等一下、等一下」，可以用：just a second、just a moment、just a minute、hold on 等句子，如：A: May I have a cup of latte? B: Just a second. / Just a moment. / Just a minute.（A：我可以來杯拿鐵嗎？B：稍等一下。）

wait a minute、wait a second、wait a moment 則比較常用在突然想起某件重要的事物時。如：Wait a minute, where is my mobile?（等一下，我的手機呢？）Wait a moment, I have an idea.（等等，我有個主意。）

❷ How can I help you? 需要幫忙嗎？

很生活化的用語，不僅僅是用在服務業，看到對方需要幫助的時候也派得上用場。一般我們會說 Can I help you?（需要幫忙嗎？）、Do you need help?（你需要幫忙嗎？），這時是看到對方面露疑惑、上前主動提供幫助。而當對方主動詢問你的時候，你可以說 How may I help you?（我可以怎麼幫你呢？）、What can I do for you?（我可以為你做什麼嗎？）。

通常我們需要／不需要幫助的時候會回答，Yes please.（好的謝謝）/ I'm good, thank you.（不用，謝謝）。

C1 ▶ Cabin Crew1 空服員 1　C2 ▶ Cabin Crew2 空服員 2
C3 ▶ Cabin Crew3 空服員 3　A ▶ All 大家

C1 ▶ Has anyone served the guy in 27D? He looks tipsy.

空服員1 ▶ 有人給 27D 的先生酒了嗎？他看起來有點醉。

C2 ▶ I served him once during the meal service.

空服員2 ▶ 我做正餐服務的時候有給過他一杯了。

C3 ▶ I served him once as well, before the service.

空服員3 ▶ 正餐服務前我給過一杯。

C1 ▶ Ok, so it's 3 in total. I think he is drunk. If he asks for drinks just delay it, alright? Let's monitor how he's doing. He is talking very loud. Make sure he is not disturbing other passengers.

A ▶ OK!

空服員1 ▶ 好,所以總共是 3 杯了,我覺得他喝醉了,如果他再跟你們要的話,就晚一點再給他,我們要隨時注意他狀況怎麼樣,他現在講話有點大聲,確保他不要影響到其他乘客。

大家 ▶ 好的。

✈ 單字解析

❶ tipsy *adj.* 喝醉的、微醺的

After 2 glasses of wine, she seems tipsy and a little bit shaky while walking.

她喝了兩杯酒之後有點微醺,走路搖搖晃晃的。

❷ drunk *adj.* 喝醉的

She hates when his father is drunk because he will talk very loud.

她很討厭父親喝醉,因為他講話會變得很大聲。

❸ delay　*v.*　延遲

I am sorry to delay the meeting, I have something urgent coming up.

很抱歉我必須延遲會議，我有急事。

❹ monitor　*v.*　監視、控管

Please monitor the oven every 10 minutes to see if the cookies are burned.

每 15 分鐘記得檢查烤箱一次，確保餅乾沒有燒焦。

❺ disturb　*v.*　打擾

Stop disturbing me. I'm working on a serious math problem.

不要吵我，我正在解一題很難的數學題目。

✈ 常用短句

❶ He looks tipsy. 他看起來有點醉。

Someone looks...（某人看起來…）。在這裡的 look 並不是表示對方看到什麼，而是表示一個人的狀態、某人看起來怎麼樣，後面接形容詞來描述他的狀態。如：She looks upset, did anything happen to her?（她看起來很沮喪，發生什麼事了嗎？）

❷ in total 總共

在結帳的時候我們常聽到 in total, in total of... 用來表示總共的數量或金額。如：There are 8 people in total you book for, right?. Yes.（訂位人數總共是八人，對嗎？是的。）意思一樣但用法不一樣的是 a total of 後面要接上數目，如：A total of 300 people are inside the auditorium.（禮堂裡面總共有三百個人。）而 total 也可以單獨當動詞使用，表示「總共」、「合計」的意思，如：The bill tonight totals to 3000 NT dollars. Let's share it!（今晚的花費總共 3000 新台幣，我們平分吧！）。

❸ make sure 確保、確認

make sure 很口語，用在提醒、叮嚀他人確定有做某事時。如：Make sure you lock the door before leaving.（出門前記得務必要鎖門。）而 be sure of / about 和 make sure 意思不一樣，不要搞混了，be sure of 表示某人對某件事物秉持著有保握、確信的態度，如：He is pretty sure that it is going to rain tonight.（他確信今天晚上會下雨）。

C1 ▸ **Cabin Crew1** 空服員 1　**C2** ▸ **Cabin Crew2** 空服員 2
C3 ▸ **Cabin Crew3** 空服員 3　**P** ▸ **Passenger** 乘客

(call bell rings)　　　　　　　　　　（服務鈴響）

P ▸ You are not giving me drinks, aren't you? I've ordered it 20 minutes ago.

乘客 ▸ 你沒有給我飲料對不對？我 20 分鐘前就要了。

C1 ▸ Yes sir, I was very busy, sorry about that. And it was just about 5 minutes ago. Give me some time, alright?

空服員1 ▸ 先生不好意思，我剛剛在忙，而且好像只過了五分鐘。給我一點時間好嗎？

P ▸ Be generous!

乘客 ▸ 大方一點嘛！

C1 ▸ Guys, I went to that passenger. He is totally drunk. I think he has some opinions about me right now. So I'm going to just put a few drops of the whiskey and add some water into his drink, to dilute it. He is not going to taste it anyway. Someone please bring this to him.

空服員1▸ 各位，我剛剛又去看了一下那位乘客，他真的喝醉了，而且他現在對我有點意見，我準備好飲料你們端過去好嗎？我會倒一些威士忌再加水，把飲料稀釋掉，以他醉的程度他應該嚐不出來，你們誰可以幫我端過去？

C2 ▸ I will do it. No problem.

空服員2▸ 我來端，沒問題！

單字解析

❶ generous　*adj.*　大方的

She is so generous that everyone in the office got her souvenir from her vacation.

她超級大方，辦公室的每個人都收到她度假帶回來的紀念品。

❷ totally　*adv.*　完全地

I totally agree with you on the ideas of sharing the bill.

我完全同意你想要分開付費的想法。

❸ dilute　*v.*　稀釋

She diluted the apple juice because it was too sweet.

她把蘋果汁稀釋，因為太甜了。

✈ 常用短句

❶ Give me some time. 等我一下／給我一些時間

Give me some time 使用的範圍很廣，沒有特定這個 time 是多長的時間，可以用在請對方給你一些時間做、想某件事，如：Could you please give me some more time, I will hand the draft to you next week!（可以再給我一些時間嗎？我下個禮拜把稿件寄給你！）也可以統稱「等一下」，如：Hurry up, we are going to be late. / Wait! Give me some time.（快點，我們要遲到了。／等等！等我一下。）

❷ have opinion on 對某人／事有意見

opinion 意見、看法，對某件事物或人有意見的話我們可以用 "have opinion on..." 來表示，如：She has opinion on that painting. She doesn't like it that much.（她對那幅畫有意見，她不怎麼喜歡。）另外，用來表示自己的看法我們可以用 "In my opinion"（在我看來、我認為），如：In my opinion, he is just trying to persuade people into buy something not really thinking from your side.（在我看來，他只是想要說服別人買東西而已，不是真心為你著想。）

C▸ Cabin Crew 空服員　P▸ Passenger 乘客

(cabin crew announcement)　（空服員廣播）

C▸ Ladies and gentlemen, the cabin crew will be giving out the forms which you need to complete before entering the customs. It is a mandatory requirement to fill it out both the declaration and customs form before entering the country.

空服員▸各位先生小姐，空服員即將會發送表格給大家。入境表格以及申報單都是在通過海關前必須要填寫的表格。請大家再入境前務必完成。謝謝。

C▸ Customs form? Does anyone need a customs form?

空服員▸入境單？有人要入境單嗎？

P▸ Excuse me, what is that?

乘客▸請問那是什麼？

C▶ A customs form. Do you need one?

空服員▶ 入境表格，你需要一張嗎？

P▶ No thanks, I have visa entering ABC already.

乘客▶ 喔喔我不需要，我有進入 ABC 國家的簽證了。

C▶ Are you holding a ABC's passport?

空服員▶ 你拿的是 ABC 的護照嗎？

P▶ No.

乘客▶ 不是。

C▶ Umm... having a visa or not doesn't matter, as long as you're entering ABC. You need to fill out this form.

空服員▶ 嗯…這跟有沒有簽證無關喔，只要你進入這個國家就要填寫入境表格。

P▶ I got it, thanks!

乘客▶ 我知道了，謝謝！

單字解析

❶ complete *v.* 完成

Please complete the task before going to school.

請在上學前完成任務。

❷ mandatory *adj.* 必要的、義務的

Mandatory military service is required in Taiwan.

服兵役在台灣是義務。

➢ military service 兵役

❸ requirement *n.* 要求

According to the requirement for promotion, you have to have less then 10 sick days in a year.

根據升遷的要求，一年內你必須少於 10 天的病假。

❹ border *n.* 國界

The enemy enter the border when they are sleeping.

敵人在他們睡著的時候入侵了國界。

✈ 常用短句

❶ give out 發送

give out 可以用在我們發送東西時，發送文件、飲料、食物等等，如：My staff will be giving out some drinks. It's our treat today.（我的員工即將會發送一些飲料招待大家。）另外，distribute 也可以表示分發的意思，如：She distributes the advertisement to everyone on the street.（她在街上發傳單給每個人。）

❷ as long as 只要

as long as 用在有前提情況下的句子，表示「只要」。如：As long as you finish your homework, you can do whatever you want.（只要你把功課做完，你要做什麼都可以。）as long as 也可以表示長達的時間，如：I can guitar as long as I want.（我彈多久的吉他都可以。）as long as 如果是用在比較級，表示「和…一樣長（長度）」，如：My hair is as long as yours.（我的頭髮和你一樣長）。

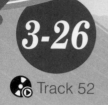

3-26 入境卡 Customs Form-2

Track 52

C ▶ Cabin Crew 空服員　P ▶ Passenger 乘客

P ▶ Sorry, what should I fill in this blank?

乘客 ▶ 不好意思，請問這格要填什麼？

C ▶ Your occupation? Oh, it's what you do for a living.

空服員 ▶ 職業？哦哦，就是您的工作！

P ▶ What about this, document number?

乘客 ▶ 這個勒?document number？

C ▶ It's your passport number.

空服員 ▶ 這是您的護照號碼。

P ▶ Surname?

乘客 ▶ Surname？

C▸ That's your last name. Your family name.

空服員 ▸ 這是您的姓氏。

P▸ What about this one? (pointing to the declaration form)

乘客 ▸ 那這張勒？（指著申報單）

C▸ That's the declaration form. You must complete it before Customs as well. You just need to tick yes or no after the questions. It's about what you carry into the country.

空服員 ▸ 這是申報單，一樣要在入海關前填寫完畢。這是關於您攜帶什麼東西入境，您只要在問題後面勾「是」或「否」就好了。

P▸ Do you think it's fine to carry fruit?

乘客 ▸ 你覺得可以帶水果進去嗎？

C▸ I don't think so. You should consume it before entering.

空服員 ▸ 應該是不行，您要在入海關前處理掉。

P▸ Cool, thanks!

乘客 ▸ 我知道了，謝謝！

1 招考資訊

2 100%應試準備教戰

3 空服員飛行英語日記

4 附錄

✈ 單字解析

❶ blank　*n.*　空格

There are lots of blanks here, where should I sign?

這麼多空格我要簽哪裡？

❷ occupation　*n.*　職業

Do you mind telling me your occupation?

你介意告訴我你的職業嗎？

❸ surname　*n.*　姓氏

Chinese surname is usually at the beginning of the name.

中文的姓氏通常擺在名字前面。

❹ declaration　*n.*　申報

You need to fill out the declaration form before entering the customs.

在過海關前你必須填寫入境申報單。

❺ tick　*v.*　勾選

Please tick the relationship status on the form.

請在婚姻狀態欄勾選目前的狀態。

❻ consume　*v.*　消耗

They consume a lot of paper cups during party.

他們在派對上用了很多紙杯。

✈ 常用短句

❶ fill in / out / up 填寫

在填寫表格的時候我們可以用 fill out，也可以說 fill in，兩者都可以表示填寫表格，只是如果要表示填寫空格，用 fill in 比較適當。如：Please fill your name in the blank.（請在空格內寫上你的姓名。）；Fill out the health form and hand it to the counter please.（填寫完健檢表格後請交給櫃台。）

另外，fill in 也有「代替某人」的意思，如：I need someone to fill in when I'm on leave.（我需要有人在我放年假時填補我的位子。）fill someone in on something 則表示和某人說某件事情，Please fill me in on what happened lately.（請告訴我最近發生了什麼事情。）

❷ What do you do for living? 你的工作是什麼？

在和別人聊天的時候常會被問到在做什麼工作，而外國人常常用 "What do you do for a living?" 問你的工作是什麼，如：What do you do for a living? I'm a teacher in high school.（你的工作是什麼？／我是高中老師。）而我們常聽到的 What do you do? 是 What do you do for living 的簡化問法。在回答時我們用 "I am＋職業"，如：I am a journalist.（我是記者。）

特別注意的是，What is your job 的意思雖然也是問別人的職業，但在國外很少人會這樣問，幾乎沒人會這樣問，這種問法太直接到讓人覺得唐突、冒犯。因此之後在與別人交談時，千萬不要用這種問法問別人的工作是什麼，對方可能會被嚇到。

行李延誤 Delayed Luggage

Track 53

C ▶ Cabin Crew 空服員　　P ▶ Passenger 乘客

C ▶ Hi, are you Ms. Lin? How are you?

空服員 ▶ 哈囉，請問是林小姐嗎？您好嗎？

P ▶ Yes, I am.

乘客 ▶ 對。

C ▶ Ok, This is what happened. I heard from the purser that one of your bags has been left behind and wasn't put in the cargo on this flight. We apologize about that. You have two pieces of luggage, right?

空服員 ▶ 我跟您說明一下發生什麼事。我從座艙長那得知，您的其中一件行李沒有送到這台飛機上，真的很抱歉，你有兩件行李對吧？

P ▶ I only have one.

乘客 ▶ 我只有一件。

C ▶ Ok, because of negligence and a misconnection, your luggage wasn't delivered on this flight. Now

空服員 ▶ 好，我知道了，因為聯繫的疏失，您的行李被遺落在我們起飛的機

what we can do is put your luggage on the same flight tomorrow. So it will reach Sao Paulo at the same time tomorrow that we land today. We would like you to provide the address for where you want the luggage to be delivered.

P ▸ But I don't have the address.

C ▸ Do you have the name of the hotel?

P ▸ I don't know that either. We are a travel group and we will only meet our guide at the airport; therefore, we don't have any information yet.

C ▸ I see. How long will you stay at that hotel?

場。我們現在會做的是：我們會把你的行李放在明天的同樣這班班機上，所以您的行李會跟著明天的班機一起抵達聖保羅。時間大概是我們等一下降落的時間。我們想請您提供您想把行李送到的地址。

乘客 ▸ 可是我不知道我們住的地址欸。

空服員 ▸ 您知道您們待在哪個飯店嗎？

乘客 ▸ 這個我也不知道，因為我們是一個旅行團，我們到了聖保羅之後才會跟導遊碰面，所以我們現在沒有任何資訊。

空服員 ▸ 我了解，您們會在那間飯店待多久？

P ▸ Only one night. The next day we are going to take another flight to Rio.

乗客 ▸ 一個晚上而已，第二天我們會搭飛機到里約。

C ▸ I understand. Would it be better for you to pick up your bag at the airport before your next flight tomorrow?

空服員 ▸ 好的，因為您們明天還有班機，如果在機場領行李對你來說會不會比較方便？

P ▸ That sounds great.

乗客 ▸ 應該會。

C ▸ Great! We will keep your luggage at the airport then. Can I have your contact number and email please?

空服員 ▸ 太好了！那我們保管您的行李，到時您到機場來領就可以了。方便留一下您的聯絡號碼和信箱嗎？

P ▸ It's 000-0000-000.

乗客 ▸ 000-0000-000。

C ▸ Thank you. After we land, could you please stay on the aircraft for a few minutes? There will be ground staff coming to give you more details.

空服員 ▸ 謝謝，等下我們降落之後可以請您先留在座位上嗎？等下會有地勤人員來告訴您更多詳細的資訊。

P ▶ Ok. 　　　　　　　　　　　　　乘客 ▶ 好的。

C ▶ Thank you so much. Once again, 　空服員 ▶ 真的很謝謝您。
we apologize for the inconvenience 　造成您的不方便我們再次
we caused. 　　　　　　　　　　　道歉。

✈ 單字解析

❶ cargo *n.* 貨物

There is a limit for cargo; therefore, there will be limit for our suitcases as well.

飛機的貨物有重量限制，因此我們的行李也會有重量限制。

❷ deliver *v.* 運送

The furniture is going to be delivered this afternoon.

家具今天下午會送來。

❸ guide *n.* 導遊

Our guide is local, so he took us to many amazing restaurants.

我們的導遊是當地人，他帶我們去很多很棒的餐廳。

❹ Rio *n.* 里約

The flight from Sao Paulo to Rio is around an hour.

從聖保羅到里約的班機大概一小時。

1 招考資訊

2 100%應試準備教戰

3 空服員飛行英語日記

4 附錄

❺ apologize   *v.*   道歉

Apologize to your sister for hitting her.

跟你妹妹道歉，因為你打她。

🛫 常用短句

❶ What's going on? 發生什麼事？

What's going on？有兩種用法，第一是問人家發生什麼事情了，比如說你剛到一個現場，不知道之前發生什麼事你就可以說 What's going on (here)？，等於 What happened 的意思。另外也可以用在打招呼的時候，等同於 What's up 的意思。如：Hey, long time no see, what's going on？（嘿，好久不見了，最近如何啊？）

❷ This is what happens(ed). （接下來要講）發生什麼事了

This is what happens(ed) 可以用在兩種情境，第一是你要告訴別人剛剛發生了什麼事情，你可以在解釋之前加上這句，或是在解釋完剛剛發生什麼事之後，把這句話放在最後，表示「以上」、「這就是剛剛發生的事情」表示你說完了。

另一種情況是用在「事情總是這樣子發展」的情境，比如你每次沒帶雨傘就會下雨，可以說 This is how it happens, whenever I forget my umbrella, it rains.（每次都這樣，只要我不帶傘，就一定會下雨）。

❸ left behind 被遺忘

left 被遺留、behind 後面，被遺留在後面，表示東西被遺忘或被遺留，可以使用在人也可用在事物上。如：She was left behind by the team in the hotel.（她被團隊遺忘在飯店了。）；My umbrella was left behind in the book store.（我的傘忘在書店忘了拿。）

❹ once again 再一次

once again（再一次）在此情境的用法表示強調的意思，Once again, we apologize for the inconvenience we caused.（造成你的不便我們再次道歉。）

除了用在道歉的場合之外，也可以用在其他需要被「強調」的情境，如：Once again, please put away your phone while the ceremony is going on.（再次聲明，在典禮期間請不要使用手機。）

3-28 失物招領 Lost And Found-1

Track 54

C ▸ Cabin Crew 空服員　P ▸ Passenger 乘客

(Cabin crew announcement)　　　　　　（空服員廣播）

C ▸ Ladies and gentlemen, we have found a ring in the lavatory. If any of you have lost a ring, please inform our cabin crew.

空服員 ▸ 各位先生小姐，我們在廁所裡發現了一枚戒指，如果您有遺失戒指，請向我們的空服人員詢問。

P ▸ Hi excuse me, I lost my ring. I was wondering if someone had pick it up and give it to you.

乘客 ▸ 不好意思，我的戒指不見了，我在想會不會有人撿到拿給你們。

C ▸ Where did you lose it?

空服員 ▸ 您掉在哪裡呢？

P ▸ I'm not really sure. I left it somewhere...

乘客 ▸ 我不太確定，應該是掉在某處…

C ▶ It's alright. What does your ring look like?

空服員 ▶ 沒關係，您的戒指長怎樣呢？

P ▶ It's a gold one with green jade on it.

乘客 ▶ 是一個金色的戒指，上面有綠色的玉。

C ▶ I'm sorry ma'am. I'm afraid this one is not the one you are looking for. It's totally different from what you described.

空服員 ▶ 抱歉，我們撿到的這個應該不是您的，這只戒指長得和您描述的不一樣。

P ▶ Ok, thanks anyway.

乘客 ▶ 沒關係，還是謝謝。

C ▶ No worries.

空服員 ▶ 不會。

✈ 單字解析

❶ inform　*v.*　通知

She was informed that her dog passed away.

她被通知她的狗去世了。

❷ jade　*n.*　玉

She has a whole wall collection of jades.

她收集了一整面牆的玉。

❸ describe　*v.*　形容、描述

Please describe the appearance of your lost wallet.

請形容你遺失錢包的外觀。

✈ **常用短句**

❶ look for 尋找

look for「尋找」可以用在尋找遺失的東西、尋找資訊、人、地點等等，如：I'm looking for my glasses, have you seen it?（我在找我的眼鏡，你有看到嗎？）／I'm looking for Jane, where is she?（我找珍妮，她到底在哪裡？）。另外，look for 也可以用在尋找工作上面，如：She is looking for a job lately. That's why she's busy.（她最近因為在找工作很忙。）

除了尋找的意思之外，look for 也能當「期望」的意思使用，如：I don't look for the bonus perk this year.（我並不期待今年的紅利。）

Track 55

C ▶ Cabin Crew 空服員   **P** ▶ Passenger 乘客

P ▶ Sorry, I lost my ring. I think I might leave it in the lavatory, but I'm not sure.

乘客 ▶ 抱歉，我的戒指不見了，我猜我可能掉在廁所裡但我不確定。

C ▶ What does it look like?

空服員 ▶ 您的戒指長怎麼樣呢？

P ▶ It's inside a dark blue box. It is a silver one with no pattern on it, but a letter "w" is on it. It is really important to me. It is engaged ring for my girlfriend.

乘客 ▶ 它是一個銀色的戒指，沒有任何圖案只有一個字母 W，然後是裝在一個暗藍色的小盒子裡。這對我來說真的很重要，它其實是我的求婚戒指…

C ▶ There you go sir. Are you looking for this one?

空服員 ▶ 嗯，在這裡，您要找的是這個吧？

P ▶ Oh my God, thank you so so so much. I cannot imagine how things will be without this little thing.

乘客 ▶ 對！天啊，太感謝你了，沒有這個我就慘了。

C ▶ No worries. Good luck for the proposal!

空服員 ▶ 沒問題，祝您求婚成功！

(During disembarkation)

（乘客下機時）

C ▶ Excuse me, sir! You cannot reenter the aircraft.

空服員 ▶ 不好意思先生！您不能再回到飛機裡！

P ▶ Oh, sorry. I forgot my phone. I just want to go to my seat to see if I left it there.

乘客 ▶ 噢抱歉，我手機忘在位子上了，可以去拿嗎？

C ▶ I'm sorry sir, but you cannot enter the aircraft again once you have disembarked No problem, just tell me your seat number and what your cell phone looks like. I will take a look for you.

空服員 ▶ 抱歉，下機之後就不能再進入機艙了。不過沒關係，跟我說您的座位號碼還有您的手機長怎樣，我去幫您找找看。

P ▶ It is an iPhone, black. My seat is 36G.

乘客 ▶ 是一支黑色的 Iphone，我的位子是 36G。

C ▶ Is it this one?

空服員 ▶ 是這支嗎？

P ▶ Yes it is! Thank you so much.

乘客 ▶ 對！謝謝你！

C ▶ No problem! Have a nice day!

空服員 ▶ 不會，保重！

單字解析

❶ proposal　*n.*　求婚

His proposal was at the beach on their vacation to Maldives.

他在馬爾地夫的海灘上求婚。

❷ reenter　*v.*　重返

He reenter the university for military reason.

他因為兵役因素重返大學。

✈ 常用短句

❶ cannot imagine... 無法想像…

imagine 表示「想像、猜測」，cannot imagine「無法想像」通常用在表示無法想像事情會如此發生，或是不希望某件事情發生。如：I cannot imagine the days without you.（我無法想像沒有你的生活）。

❷ Wish you good luck on... 祝你好運…

我們在和別人聊天過後除了可以說 Have a nice day！之外，也可以針對聊天的內容決定要不要說 Wish you good luck.，表示祝福對方做某件事情時能夠順利，同樣代表在對話結束後一種禮貌性的祝福。I am going to see my manager next week. / Wish you good luck.（我下禮拜要去見我的經理／祝你好運）。通常我們說 Wish you good luck 即可，如果要針對某件事情祝福對方的話則用「on」來連接要祝福的事情。如：Wish you good luck on your exam!（祝你考試順利！）

❸ in... color 某物品為…顏色

要說某種東西為某個顏色的時候，我們用「in」表示，如：My car is blue in color.（我的車子是藍色的。）我們要表示穿著的時候也適用「in」這個介系詞，如：My sister is the one in the cap.（我姊姊是戴著帽子的那位。）

1 招考資訊

2 100%應試準備教戰

3 空服員飛行英語日記

4 附錄

附錄

✈ 國際城市、機場代碼中英對照

機場代碼	國家COUNTRY	城市CITY	機場名稱
TPE	台灣	台北	桃園中正機場
KHH	台灣	高雄	
HND	日本	東京	羽田機場
NRT	日本	東京	成田機場
KIX	日本	大阪	
NGO	日本	名古屋	
ICN	南韓	首爾	仁川機場
PEK	中國	北京	
CAN	中國	廣州	
HKG	中國	香港	
PVG	中國	上海	浦東機場
MNL	菲律賓	馬尼拉	
KUL	馬來西亞	吉隆坡	
SIN	新加坡	新加坡	樟宜機場
BKK	泰國	曼谷	
CGK	印尼	雅加達	
DPS	印尼	峇里島	
BOM	印度	孟買	
CCU	印度	加爾各答	
SGN	越南	胡志明市	
HAN	越南	河內	

PNH	柬埔寨	金邊	
AUH	阿拉伯聯合大公國	阿布達比	
DXB	阿拉伯聯合大公國	杜拜	
DME	俄羅斯	莫斯科	
DHA	沙烏地阿拉伯	達蘭	
BNE	澳洲	布里斯本	
MEL	澳洲	墨爾本	
PER	澳洲	伯斯	
SYD	澳洲	雪梨	
AKL	紐西蘭	奧克蘭	
CHC	紐西蘭	基督城	
WLG	紐西蘭	威靈頓	
JFK	美國	紐約	甘迺迪機場
LGA	美國	紐約	拉瓜迪亞機場
EWR	美國	紐約	紐瓦克自由機場
ATL	美國	亞特蘭大	
BOS	美國	波士頓	
ORD	美國	芝加哥	
DFW	美國	達拉斯	
IAH	美國	休士頓	
LAX	美國	洛杉磯	
MIA	美國	邁阿密	
SFO	美國	舊金山	
SEA	美國	西雅圖	
HNL	美國	檀香山	
IAD	美國	華盛頓特區	
YVR	加拿大	溫哥華	

YOW	加拿大	渥太華	
YYZ	加拿大	多倫多	
YUL	加拿大	蒙特婁	
MEX	墨西哥	墨西哥市	
RIO	巴西	里約熱內盧	
GRU	巴西	聖保羅	
SJU	波多黎哥	聖胡安	
BUE	阿根廷	布宜諾斯艾利斯	
LIM	秘魯	利馬	
VIE	奧地利	維也納	
LUX	盧森堡	盧森堡	
HEL	芬蘭	赫爾辛基	
OSL	挪威	奧斯陸	
ZRH	瑞士	蘇黎世	
GVA	瑞士	日內瓦	
LGW	英國	倫敦	蓋威特機場
LHR	英國	倫敦	希斯洛機場
LCY	英國	倫敦	倫敦城市機場
MAN	英國	曼徹斯特	
DUB	愛爾蘭	都柏林	
CDG	法國	巴黎	
LYS	法國	里昂	
MAD	西班牙	馬德里	
BCN	西班牙	巴賽隆納	
LIS	葡萄牙	里斯本	
FRA	德國	法蘭克福	

DUS	德國	杜賽爾道夫	
MUC	德國	慕尼黑	
AMS	荷蘭	阿姆斯特丹	
CPH	丹麥	哥本哈根	
FCO	義大利	羅馬	
MXP	義大利	米蘭	
VCE	義大利	威尼斯	
ARN	瑞典	斯德哥爾摩	
ATH	希臘	雅典	
BRU	比利時	布魯塞爾	

國內外航空公司IATA代碼及中英文全名

A	AA美國航空American Airlines
	AC加拿大航空Air Canada
	AE華信航空Mandarin Airlines
	AF法國航空Air France
	AI印度航空Air India
	AY芬蘭航空Finn Air
B	B7立榮航空 Uni Air
	BA英國航空British Airways
	BG孟加拉航空Biman Airlines
	BI汶萊皇家航空Royal Brunei Airlines
	BR長榮航空EVA Air
C	CA中國國際航空Air China
	CI中華航空China Airlines
	CX國泰航空Cathay Pacific Airways
	CZ中國南方航空China Southern Airlines
D	DL美國達美航空Delta Airlines
E	EK阿聯酋航空公司Emirates
F	FE遠東航空Far Eastern Air Transport
G	GA印尼嘉魯達航空Garuda Indonesia (The Airlines of Indonesia)
	GE復興航空TransAsia Airways
J	JL日本航空Japan Airlines
K	KA港龍航空Dragonair
	KE大韓航空Korean Air
	KL荷蘭皇家航空Royal Dutch Airlines

L	LH德國漢莎航空Lufthansa German Airlines
M	MH馬來西亞航空Malaysia Airlines
	MU中國東方航空公司China Eastern Airlines
N	NH全日空航空All Nippon Airways (ANA)
	NZ紐西蘭航空Air New Zealand
O	OZ韓亞航空公司Asiana Airlines
P	PR菲律賓航空Philippine Airlines
Q	QF澳洲航空Qantas Airways
	QR卡達航空Qatar Airways
R	RA尼泊爾航空公司Nepal Airlines
	RJ皇家約旦航空Royal Jordanian Airlines
S	SA南非航空South African Airways
	SQ新加坡航空 Singapore Airlines
	SU俄羅斯航空Aeroflot Russian Airlines
T	TG泰國航空Thai Airways
	TK土耳其航空Turkish Airlines
U	UA美國聯合航空United Airlines
V	VN越南航空公司Vietnam Airlines
	VS維珍航空Virgin Atlantic Airways

1 招考資訊

2 100%應試準備教戰

3 空服員飛行英語日記

4 附錄

常見特別餐代碼參考表

特別餐代碼	特別餐英文	特別餐中文
AVML	ASIAN VEGETARIAN MEAL	亞洲素食
BBML	INFANT/BABY FOOD	嬰兒餐
BLML	BLAND MEAL	溫和餐
CHML	CHILD MEAL	兒童餐
DBML	DIABETIC MEAL	糖尿病餐
FPML	FRUIT PLATTER	水果餐
GFML	GLUTEN FREE MEAL	麩質不耐症餐
HNML	HINDU (NON VEGETARIAN) MEAL	非素食印度餐
JPML	JAPANESE MEAL	日式餐
KSML	KOSHER MEAL	猶太餐
LCML	LOW CALORIE MEAL	低卡路里餐
LFML	LOW CHOLESTEROL/LOW FAT MEAL	低脂肪／膽固醇餐
LSML	LOW SODIUM, NO SALT ADDED	低鹽無鹽餐
MOML	MOSLEM MEAL	回教餐
NLML	NON LACTOSE	低乳糖餐
PWML	POST WEANING MEAL	斷奶餐
RVML	RAW VEGETARIAN MEAL	生菜餐
SFML	SEAFOOD MEAL	海鮮餐
SUMML	SEMI-FLUID MEAL	半流質餐
VJML	VEGETARIAN JAIN MEAL	耆那素食
VGML	VEGAN MEAL (NON-DAIRY)	西方（嚴格）素食

VLML	VEGETARIAN MEAL (LACTO-OVO)	蛋奶素食
VOML	VEGETARIAN ORIENTAL MEAL	東方素食

世界常用流通貨幣代碼

代碼	英文	中文
AED	United Arab Emirates Dirham	阿聯酋迪拉姆
AUD	Australian Dollar	澳元
CAD	Canadian Dollar	加拿大元
EUR	Euro	歐元
GBP	Pound Sterling	英鎊
HKD	Hong Kong Dollar	港元
JPY	Japanese Yen	日圓
KRW	Korean Won	韓圜
MYR	Malaysian Ringgit	馬來西亞令吉
NZD	New Zealand Dollar	紐西蘭元
PHP	Philippines Peso	菲律賓披索
RMB	Chinese Renminbi	人民幣
SAR	Saudi Arabia Riyal	里亞爾
SGD	Singapore Dollar	新加坡幣
THB	Thai Baht	泰國銖
TWD	New Taiwan Dollar	新台幣
USD	United States Dollar	美元

✈ 歐洲申根區國家

　　申根區是指根據 1985 年在盧森堡申根鎮簽署的《申根協議》所形成的一個類似單獨國家的區域，其中包含歐洲國家如下。旅客在進出這個區域時，只需在其中一個國家入境後，能在區域內的組成國家自由進出，再由任何一個國家出境。現在中華民國護照持有者到歐洲各國雖然免簽證，但申根區和非申根區的停留時間卻有些許差異。在申根區總停留日數會合併計算，每 6 個月期間內最多總共能停留 90 天。其他非申根區的國家則分別計算其停留日數。

申根區組成國一覽表 as of 2013
安道爾 Andorra
奧地利 Austria
比利時 Belgium
捷克 Czech Republic
丹麥 Denmark
愛沙尼亞 Estonia
丹麥法羅群島 Faroe Islands
芬蘭 Finland
法國 France
德國 Germany
希臘 Greece
丹麥格陵蘭島 Greenland
教廷 The Holy See
匈牙利 Hungary

冰島 Iceland

義大利 Italy

拉脫維亞 Latvia

列支敦斯登 Liechtenstein

立陶宛 Lithuania

盧森堡 Luxembourg

馬爾他 Malta

摩納哥 Monaco

荷蘭 Netherlands

挪威 Norway

波蘭 Poland

葡萄牙 Portugal

聖馬利諾 San Marino

斯洛伐克 Slovakia

斯洛維尼亞 Slovenia

西班牙 Spain

瑞典 Sweden

瑞士 Switzerland

【資料來源：外交部網站及維基百科】

1 招考資訊

2 100%應試準備教戰

3 空服員飛行英語日記

4 附錄

Learn Smart! 061

Flight Attendant

夢想啟航：空服員的英文應試+飛行日誌 (MP3)

作　　者	胡夢瑋
發 行 人	周瑞德
執行總監	齊心瑀
企劃編輯	陳欣慧
執行編輯	魏于婷
校　　對	編輯部
封面構成	高鍾琪

內頁構成	菩薩蠻數位文化有限公司
印　　製	大亞彩色印刷製版股份有限公司
初　　版	2016 年 8 月
定　　價	新台幣 380 元
出　　版	倍斯特出版事業有限公司
電　　話	(02) 2351-2007
傳　　真	(02) 2351-0887
地　　址	100 台北市中正區福州街 1 號 10 樓之 2
E - m a i l	best.books.service@gmail.com
網　　址	www.bestbookstw.com

港澳地區總經銷	泛華發行代理有限公司
地　　　　址	香港新界將軍澳工業邨駿昌街 7 號 2 樓
電　　　　話	(852) 2798-2323
傳　　　　真	(852) 2796-5471

國家圖書館出版品預行編目資料

```
Flight Attendant 夢想啟航：空服員的英文
應試+飛行日誌 / 胡夢瑋著. -- 初版. -- 臺
北市：倍斯特，2016.08
  面；　公分. --（Learn smart！；61）
ISBN 978-986-92855-5-1(平裝附光碟片)

1.英語 2.航空勤務員 3.讀本

    805.18    105012996
```